Collision with Chronos

Books by Barrington Bayley

Annihilation Factor
Collision with Chronos
Empire of Two Worlds
The Fall of Chronopolis
The Forest of Peldain
The Garments of Caean
The Great Hydration
The Grand Wheel
The Knights of the Limits (short story collection)
The Pillars of Eternity
The Rod of Light
The Seed of Evil (short story collection)
The Sinners of Erspia
The Soul of the Robot
Star Virus
Star Winds
The Zen Gun

Collision with Chronos

Barrington Bayley

Cosmos Books, an imprint of **Wildside Press**
New Jersey . New York . California . Ohio

Collision with Chronos

Published by:

Cosmos Books, an imprint of Wildside Press
P.O. Box 45, Gillette, NJ 07933-0045
www.wildsidepress.com

For more information, contact Wildside Press.

ISBN: 1-58715-380-7

1.

Rond Heshke wondered if there would ever be victory without arrogance. Banners, everywhere banners.

On the raised forecourt of Bupolbloc, world headquarters of the Bureau of Politics, they hung to form a gigantic grill, like an array of sails a hundred feet tall. Even though the last of the wars against the deviant subspecies -- the campaign against the Amhraks - had been won twenty years before, these banners were still redolent of military glory. And still there were the annual parades, the rousing speeches, the braying documentaries on the vidcast.

The War to Win Earth: that was what they had called it. But now Earth was won - irrevocably won for True Man - and privately Heshke thought it was time the paean of triumph was played down.

He crossed the forecourt, intimidated by the immense red-and-black canvases, which swallowed up all visitors like ants. In point of fact Bupolbloc was the most impressive of the many fine buildings in the administrative sector of Pradna, soaring up for over a thousand feet of serried glass frontages, and it exuded a sense of power that soon overshadowed Heshke's disrespectful thoughts, making them seem sacrilegious. He entered the spacious foyer and checked his destination on the office plan.

He took an elevator to the twentieth floor and then walked through seemingly endless corridors. All around him passed the tall, handsome men and women of the Titanium Legions, the self-styled Guardians of Earth who currently had succeeded in attaining political supremacy over humanity. Wearing sleek uniforms in black and gold, all of impeccable biological pedigree, they cast disdainful glances at Heshke which he chose not to notice. He accepted that any military elite was apt to revel in its own superiority; he was, after all, but a paunchy, middle-aged civilian

5

who, insofar as anyone could these days, took no interest in politics. His concern was with the past, not the future.

The twentieth floor lay in the precinct of the Bureau of Propaganda and the office he had been summoned to was the Archaeological Office – Bureprop (Arch.). He arrived in good time and was kept waiting only ten minutes by the pretty, coolly efficient secretary before being ushered in.

Titan-Major Brourne rose to greet him, smiling jovially.

"Good to see you, Citizen Heshke! Sit down, won't you?"

Behind Brourne stood a younger man Heshke did not know: a pale, supercilious-looking captain with a deformed left eyelid – an unlikely defect to find in a Titan, and which gave him a disconcerting, quizzical expression. Heshke could only suppose that he made up for the deformity in other qualities, or he would never have been permitted to enter the ranks of the Titans.

"This is Titan-Captain Brask, Citizen," Brourne said by way of introduction. "I've called him to our meeting for reasons which will become plain later." He sat down and leaned back, placing his large hands squarely on the table. Brourne was a solid-looking man, somewhat too broad for his height, and his tub-like bulkiness was accentuated by the crossed black belts of his uniform. He had thinning brown hair that had once been thick and luxurious, brown eyes and a face that, having seen much and enjoyed much, was now beginning to soften under a new career of desk-work. Heshke preferred him brisk and businesslike rather than jovial, as now. His cordiality always was an introduction to something else.

Heshke's gaze drifted to an archaeological chart that covered the wall behind the two men. It was a good professional piece of work, even if too much biased in favour of the particular interpretations the Titans put upon historical findings. It clearly showed the periodic rise and fall of civilisation, the persistent pattern of all human history. He was still staring at it when Titan-Major Brourne spoke again.

"Well, Citizen, and how is progress at the ruins?"

"I can't speak of any new developments, if that's what you mean." Heshke fumbled uneasily with his briefcase.

The Titan-Major's voice became heavy and unaccommodating. "What you're trying to tell me is that there's been no progress."

"You can't always depend on progress to follow a straight line," Heshke answered defensively. "The first thing to learn about the alien interventionists is how complete their destruction was, how nearly all their traces were erased. In a sense we are lucky that sites like the Hathar Ruins exist at all."

Brourne rose from his desk and paced to and fro, his face becoming serious. "Victory is ours, but it must be consolidated," he intoned. "The history of the Fall and of the Dark Period must be fully researched and documented, if we are going to be able to give future generations a correct historical perspective."

Titan-Captain Brask continued to gaze on the scene as if from some superior viewpoint while Brourne held forth. "We've beaten the deviant subspecies – but they were always the lesser threat. I don't have to tell you what the greater threat is, or how crucial your own area of research is, Citizen Heshke. You know just what the nature of a future struggle would be; we must never again allow ourselves to become vulnerable to an attack from space."

He stopped pacing and looked directly at Heshke once more. "Our present ignorance is unacceptable. It has been officially decreed that progress in the research into the alien interventionists is required."

Heshke did not know how to answer him. He wished he was back at the alien ruins, quietly going about his work with his colleagues, not here in this office being browbeaten by Titan officers.

"In that case new sites will have to be unearthed," he opined. "I would go so far as to say we've already got most of what we can from Hathar." How much can they expect me to deduce, he thought, from empty stone ruins and a few nonhuman skeletons? It really was extraordinary how few artifacts had survived.

For the first time the younger Titan spoke. His voice was precise and condescending.

"We do not rely only on your efforts, Citizen. We have our own archaeological teams – and they, let me say, are producing better results than you are."

Yes, they would, Heshke thought. Because the Titans already had an ideology, a creed. It was easy to dig up a few remains and recruit them in support of already constructed doctrines. But Heshke thought of himself as a scientist and a scholar, not as an ideologist, and he took facts simply as facts. As far as the alien interventionists went there was altogether too little information to form a complete picture.

Oh, the broad outlines were clear enough, all right. About eight hundred years ago the powerful and mature classical civilisation

7

had suffered a total, cataclysmic collapse. The subsequent Dark Period had lasted nearly four centuries, and only since then had civilisation been built anew.

But it was also evident that another civilisation, not of Earth, had established itself here side by side with the human one sometime during the past thousand years. It also had been wiped out – but much, much more completely. That a civilisation could be eradicated so completely was puzzling. The actual age of the ruins it had left behind it was still in dispute, but to the ideologues of the Titanium Legions the inference was unavoidable – the old human civilisation had died in a gigantic struggle to save Earth from the intruders. Though it had succeeded in its mission, the effort had been too much for it and had left it too weak to survive.

The argument was plausible. The alien remains showed every sign of having been destroyed in furious warfare, and nearly everyone accepted that the war between the two races had taken place. But as for the second premise . . . Heshke's eyes strayed back to the archaeological chart on the wall. The collapse of classical civilisation was hardly a unique event in history. Rather there had been a whole series of such collapses at intervals separated by about two millennia, as if human civilisation were inherently incapable of supporting itself, time and time again falling under its own weight. Some extremists among the Titans attributed this pattern to successive waves of alien invasion, but there was no evidence to support the idea.

And neither, despite exhaustive efforts on the part of Heshke and numerous colleagues, was there really decisive evidence to show that the last, classical civilisation *had* in fact disappeared under the onslaught of alien attack. To Heshke's mind the picture was more one of a rapid internal decline covering about a century and culminating in final violent collapse. Furthermore, there was an inexplicable lack of reference to the aliens in most of the records so far unearthed. Nevertheless he found himself having to accept the Interventionist Theory, with some reservations, even if only on the grounds of probability. After all, the aliens had been there, and they might have used weapons whose effects were not now discernible.

He hesitated, then opened his briefcase and took out a set of glossy photographs. "I wasn't sure whether or not to show you these. They're quite interesting in a way. . . ."

He passed the photographs across the desk. Brourne and Brask bent to inspect them. They were pictures, taken from various angles, of the alien ruins where he had his camp.

"These came into my hands a short while ago," he explained diffidently. "They were passed on to me by a colleague making a study of the old town of Jejos – it's due for demolition, you know. We think they were taken about three hundred years back, probably by an amateur historian of the time. At first we thought they would be instructive; however. . . ."

He dipped into his briefcase again and passed over more photographs. "These are modern pictures, taken from the same angles for comparison."

Brourne looked from one batch to the other in puzzlement. "So?"

Heshke leaned across the desk. "See this conical tower here? Even today it's in fairly good shape, as you can see. Yet in the old photograph – the one three hundred years old – it's missing, except for a crumbled base."

Brourne snorted. "That's impossible."

"Yes, obviously," agreed Heshke. "There are other anomalies too – crumbled walls, generally deteriorated stonework; in fact if we were to believe these photographs it would mean that the ruins are in better condition – are – newer! – today than they were three hundred years ago."

"So what do you make of that?"

Heshke shrugged. "Apparently, for some reason, the pictures have been touched up and generally faked to make the ruins seem older than they were."

"And why would anyone want to do that?"

"I haven't even the beginning of an idea. But that's what must have happened. There's no other explanation."

"Obviously." Brourne's voice was sarcastic, and Heshke felt stupid for having raised the matter at all. "And that would seem to negate their historical value," the Titan-Major continued, staring intently at the pictures. Finally he handed them to Brask. "Have copies made of all these," he said.

The fakery, Heshke reminded himself, was extremely well-done. The old yellow prints gave him quite an eerie feeling.

Brourne coughed and returned his attention to Heshke. "We are wondering if you have sufficient enthusiasm for the task that has been entrusted to you?" he asked, sending a chill down

Heshke's spine. "Perhaps you fail to appreciate the urgency of what confronts us. Remember that the research you're doing has more than one motive. There is the need for scientific knowledge, of course – the need to know as much as possible about the great war our ancestors fought with the aliens, so as to give our political attitudes a firm historical basis. But there is also another reason. Already the aliens have tried to steal Earth once: who knows when they might try again? We have to know where they came from, we have to know whether they might still be lurking out there in space. *We have to know about their weapons.*"

Brask entered the conversation again. Into his icy blue eyes came a glint of steel, making their oddness all the more striking. "Have you heard the latest theories about how the deviant subspecies arose? It has always been a mystery as to why they should arise when they did, when the natural course of evolution is quite plainly in the direction of pure-blooded True Man. Radioactivity from warfare cannot be the answer, because the nuclear weapons used in the classical era were radiologically clean. Well, it has recently been discovered that the Earth's magnetic field wards off high-powered particles coming in from outer space. If this field were interfered with so as to allow the passage of these particles the rate of biological mutation on Earth would increase to an unnatural level. Such a situation is consistent with the growth of deviant species."

Heshke frowned. "But *could* Earth's magnetism be interfered with?" he asked doubtfully.

"Theoretically – yes. We don't know precisely how, but we're working on it, naturally. I think there can be little doubt what happened – the deviant subspecies are the products of an alien weapon whose object was to destroy our genetic purity – to pervert nature itself!"

Brourne nodded his agreement. "We know for a fact that not only man was involved. Several breeds of dog existing today, for instance, were not in existence a thousand years ago."

Heshke ignored this dubious item of reasoning. "If it could be established that Earth's magnetic field *did* undergo changes at the appropriate time, then that would largely substantiate the theory," he ventured. "But even then – could it not equally have been one of our *own* weapons that did it?"

Titan-Captain Brask's response to this suggestion was indignant. "Would True Man have jeopardised the blood of the future? The

10

idea is absurd, inconceivable. The interference can only have come from a nonhuman source, and the enemy that produced it may still exist, preparing himself for a fresh assault. We may yet be called upon to defend not only Earth, but our very genes!" And he fixed Heshke with an icy stare.

"And so there you have it, Citizen Heshke," Brourne resumed in a tone of deadly seriousness. "*Now* do you see why our archaeological work is of such importance?"

Wearily Heshke nodded his understanding. The endless ideologising of the Titans fatigued him, yet he had to admit the urgency of their demands. Unpleasant though their practices sometimes were, they were a necessary force.

And at the moment a chill more penetrating than their veiled threats had entered his loins. The picture of alien fingers meddling with man's genetic heritage was a vision of pure horror.

"You're right, absolutely right," he said in subdued tones. "We need to call on all our resources to meet a threat as big as this. Yet to be honest I don't see what I can do that I'm not already doing. The Hathar Ruins *are* just about played out. I don't think I can draw any more fresh conclusions without fresh evidence."

The two Titans glanced at one another. Brourne nodded, and instantly the atmosphere seemed to relax.

"We're aware of your difficulties," the Titan-Major said, "and we have some news for you. In another part of the world a discovery has been made that you don't yet know about. We want you to take part in a field trip."

A feeling of relief swept over Heshke. He was not going to be purged after all!

Traditionally suspicious of everyone, the Titans had been baiting him, sounding out his attitudes to make sure he was the right man for the job. Evidently it was something they couldn't use one of their own people for – Heshke was well aware that they would have liked to dispense with the services of civilians altogether, but they couldn't. Titan scientists, if left to their own resources, too often seemed to fall down in the last analysis, tripped up by their attachment to prejudicial theories. Heshke was the foremost authority in his field and they needed him and men like him.

Often he had wondered what he would do if, appallingly, he was offered a Titan commission. To accept or to refuse both had the aspect of suicide.

"The trip is extremely unusual in nature," Brourne continued.

11

"I must warn you that there is a certain degree of danger involved."

Heshke blinked. "Physical danger?"

"Yes. Not the sort of thing an archaeologist usually has to face, I know, but . . ." Brourne shrugged, waving his hand casually.

"No, no, not altogether." Heshke became excited. "As a profession we're always prepared – unknown regions, and all that. Where will we be going? Into a dev reservation?"

"I'm sorry, the details are top secret at the moment. You'll be briefed in good time."

It had to be a dev reservation, Heshke thought. Where on a conquered, controlled planet could there be risk to life and limb except in one of the special regions where a few surviving deviants were allowed to survive for purposes of study? The Titans must have made an important find there – perhaps a hitherto unknown alien settlement.

"Surely you can give me some indication?" he persisted. "I'd like to have some idea of what to expect."

Brourne hesitated, an unusual gesture for him. "One of our teams has found an alien artifact in good condition. In working order, in fact. It's a more significant find than anything else we've ever turned up . . . I'm afraid I can't tell you more. The truth is I'm not allowed to know much myself. But you must be prepared to be called away on short notice."

He came to his feet again, signalling that the interview was at an end. "Well there it is, Citizen, I'm glad to see you so enthusiastic. I hope we can depend on you to do your damnedest for us . . . for humanity. . . ."

Heshke rose, made a curt bow, and left.

2.

Squat conical towers.

Throughout the world these were the features of alien architecture to survive more than any other, probably by reason of being the most difficult for time or man to dismantle. The ruins Heshke and his team were studying sported plenty of them.

He arrived back at the site at sunset. The Hathar Ruins, as the site was called, was one of the most important of outworlder remains, and one of the best preserved. More typical were the expanses of fused glass where cities and settlements had been destroyed by nuclear bombardment. The Hathar Ruins had not sustained an atomic hit, but they had suffered extensive damage from less powerful weapons; nevertheless they still exuded a rich aura of a bygone race. Crumbled walls, curiously curved and rounded, wavered toward the sky. The short conical towers seemed to sprout everywhere and at all levels. It was hard to believe that the aliens had been on Earth for a comparatively short time – which had to be the case if history made any sense at all. This settlement, and even more so the larger settlements dotted around the world, were clearly built to last.

The team was just finishing its day's work of carefully sifting earth. Heshke hurried over to the finds tent, hoping to see some new artifact, perhaps even a document in the cryptic alien script that no one, so far, had deciphered. As usual, he was disappointed. In the North Sector, in the large building popularly known as the Cathedral, someone had uncovered a glass object of which there were already scores of samples. It was believed to be a common domestic article used for squashing fruit.

That, in essence, was most of what they had. Simple articles of common use, elementary tools, some furniture. From skeletons they had a fair idea of the aliens' physical appearance. But the advanced technology, the machines, equipment, records – virtually the whole apparatus of a tremendously advanced species – had all gone in the frenzy of annihilation in which the men of the past had torn through everything alien, burning and pulverising. A few rusted, mangled machines had been found, but not enough to reconstruct even approximately what the outworld technology had been like.

Heshke did not blame the men who had carried out this destruction – they had seen their planet despoiled, their society wrecked – but in retrospect it was an unintelligent move.

He could not wait to see the functional artifact that Brourne had promised.

He was watching a young teamster clean the fruit-squasher, when there was a movement behind him. He turned to see Blare Oblomot, his chief assistant.

"Well, Rond," Blare said breezily, "what did the Titans want?"

Heshke coughed, looking nervously at the teamster. He took it for granted that someone on his team was a Titan "watcher", and it made him feel uncomfortable. He jerked his head toward the exit.

"How about a drink in your place?" he said once they were outside. As they walked toward Blare's quarters he noticed that the camp seemed abnormally quiet and even Blare seemed slightly uneasy. That was odd: the tousle-haired, raffish archaeologist usually had an unshakable confidence.

Blare lifted the flap to his tent for Heshke to enter. Seated at the small wooden table, he poured them both glasses of wine.

"The Titans have been here today," he announced. "Asking questions. Practically interrogating everyone, in fact."

Heshke started. "What kind of questions?"

"Political, what else?" Blare shrugged, looking away. "You know, I think I feel the cold wind of a purge coming on. They wanted to know a lot about you, too."

Heshke put down his glass, feeling suddenly numb. So far he had managed to keep Titan influence at the site minimal. He had seen what happened when the Titans put in their own teams to work alongside civilian diggers: they soon dominated the entire project; scientific objectivity was the first casualty. He didn't want that here.

At the same time the calculating coolness of it struck him. The Titans had wanted to investigate the project while he, its leader,

14

was absent. Why?

"What did they ask about me?" he demanded.

"They seemed to want to find out whether you are . . . on their side, for lack of another way of putting it. Are you, Rond? What's going on, anyway? Are we being taken over?"

Slowly Heshke shook his head. "No . . . it's something else." He was silent for a few moments. "My God, it must be something big," he muttered wonderingly.

"What, Rond?" Blare looked at him curiously, the light of the lamp playing over his sharp features. "Well, you know my views. I don't mind telling you I had a fright today. I think I'll have to get out."

Heshke blinked. "Don't be ridiculous, Blare. There's nothing to worry about. They're checking up, that's all. They've made an important find, and they want me to help them. . . . I shouldn't really tell you anything, but hang it all, I don't really know any more than you do. They've found an alien artifact and I gather they're excited about it. Anyway, it entails a field trip. I don't know where to, except that it's probably somewhere in a dev reservation."

Blare was frowning. "Really? Why only probably?"

"Well, there's some danger involved. That's all they would tell me."

Blare grunted. "Dev reservations are pretty quiet places these days, you know, except for when the Titans go storming in. You may not be going to one."

"Well, perhaps not. I just wanted to reassure you that there's no purge coming, that's all."

"Thanks for your concern, Rond, but . . . I still think I'd better go. I got the impression this afternoon that something more is brewing. I don't feel safe here any more."

Heshke stared at him. "What on Earth are you talking about, Blare?"

The other moved uneasily and took a gulp of wine. The movements of his head cast grotesque shadows on the canvas of the tent, the lamp being set on the table beside them.

"I'd better be frank – hang it, I feel I can trust *you*, if no one else. You know my sympathies – you know there's a political opposition. I think the Titans are on to me, and if so you know what the outlook will be if I hang around much longer."

"*On* to you?" Heshke echoed uncomprehendingly. "But of

course there's a political opposition – there always is! It's hardly a crime to belong to it. Not unless you mean . . ."

His voice trailed off. He had known Blare Oblomot for years. Like Heshke himself, he was one of the foremost experts in his field, though younger and less experienced. Heshke also knew of his contempt for the Titans, of his somewhat anarchistic-liberal views. But he had always put that down to a kind of freakish way-wardness – no, not freakish, he corrected himself hastily; freakish was an unfortunate word – to a kind of charming and frivolous individuality. But not as a serious defiance of . . .

His thoughts, like his voice, trailed off.

Blare was speaking wryly. "There's always a point where opposition becomes incompatible with good citizenship. What is legitimate, even if disapproved of, in peacetime becomes treasonable in a state of war. Figuratively speaking we're still in a state of war. So there comes a time when one has to make a hard and cut decision. I made mine some time ago." Blare rubbed the side of his face. Heshke noticed the fatigue in his eyes – did the Titans have that effect on *him*, too?

"Blare – you're not telling me that you're one of . . . *them.*"

Oblomot nodded. "Yes, I'm afraid so. I was pushed into it step by step, really, by the Titans themselves. Their grip has tightened, not relaxed, since the Deviant Wars. Their ideas have taken an even more intransigent form, so that even some thoughts would infringe the legal code today, if there was some way to monitor thoughts. So when you belong to a secret organisation pledged to fight the Titans by any means whatsoever and which believes the *so-called* deviants should be allowed a place in the world—"

"Blare! What are you saying!"

Oblomot shrugged again. "You see? Even you can't approach a thought like that. And yet you like the Titans scarcely any more than I do."

Heshke's shoulders sagged. Here was his old friend Blare Oblomot confessing that he was a race traitor; that he was secretly a member of the despised underground that during the last war had actually *helped* the Amhraks. It just didn't bear thinking about; his bewilderment was complete.

He forced himself to speak mildly, calmly. "One can make many criticisms of them, of course," he said, "but the Titans aren't the source of their ideology – they are merely its chief instrument. And that instrument is *necessary*, Blare. Earth has to be defend-

16

ed; so does the correct evolutionary lineage – I'm astounded if you can't see that."

"Defending Earth against an alien invader is one thing," Oblomot rejoindered. "We haven't had to do that – this civilisation hasn't had to do that. It all happened centuries ago. As for the rest —" He shook his head sadly.

Although he felt he had had enough of arguing for one day, Heshke could hardly allow such wild contentions to pass unchallenged. "But it's all part of the same thing!" he protested. "The blood that flows in the veins of the Titanium Legions is the same blood that flowed in the men who flung back the invader. The threat is the same, the task is the same – to have and to hold the planet Earth!"

He was, he knew, spouting Titan slogans, but that didn't worry him. This was part of the creed he would never seriously have doubted.

But Oblomot merely looked sardonic. "The blood in the veins of the deviant species is the same, too. We're all descended from Classical Man."

"Yes, but —"

"I know what you're going to say. That we alone carry the unchanged line of Classical Man and hence constitute True Man – the others are aberrations leading away from the 'natural' line of evolutionary development. Well, it *is* true that we're closest to Classical Man, in physical characteristics, anyway. And probably in mental characteristics too, I grant you that."

"Then there you are. That *is* what I'm saying."

"Yes, but what does it mean? Just because we resemble an old type doesn't mean that newer types are somehow wrong. I and my friends aren't opposed to evolution, Rond. We're trying to *save* evolution from being stopped, from being cut short – because that's what the Titans are doing. Nature's method is diversity – always to be radiating out into new forms. The Titans are destroying all new forms and imposing a rigid uniformity. Believe me, we'll all be victims in the end."

Heshke found these new ideas frightening. "The Titans believe the deviants were caused by an alien weapon that affected mankind's genes," he said.

"Yes, I've heard that type of theory before. Perhaps it's true. Or perhaps it was one of our own weapons. But so what? All these mutation-inducing influences can do is speed up evolution, com-

17

pressing into centuries what otherwise would have taken tens of millennia or longer. The subspecies we've been dutifully annihilating would have developed sooner or later anyway."

There was an awkward silence. Heshke shook his head, sighing deeply.

"I still say only one race can occupy the Earth," he said sombrely. "For heaven's sake, how do you expect us to react to an all-out attack by the Lorenes?"

Oblomot nodded slowly. "In that particular case, I agree with you. The Lorenes were an even more aggressive species than we are; they had to be wiped out – they were a strain this planet just couldn't afford. But we didn't stop there, we went on to all the others. The Lorenes were a danger, yes – but the Amhraks?" He smiled. "No, Rond. And as for the Urukuri, they were scarcely able to put up a fight. As a matter of fact I think it's stretching a point to call them a subspecies at all. They merely have exaggerated negroid characteristics and an exceptionally placid disposition."

"Think of the dangers of miscegenation. Of our blood becoming contaminated with Urukuri or Amhrak blood." Heshke shuddered slightly. "Imagine your daughter being raped by one. They *have* raped our women, you know."

Oblomot rummaged for a fresh bottle in a nearby cabinet. It was as if he were pretending not to hear Heshke.

At last he said heavily: "Have another drink, Rond. I don't blame you for thinking like that, because Titan propaganda is very good and everybody is infected by it. To your mind it even appears perfectly rational, that's how good it is. But it's wrong."

Sipping the newly filled glass, Heshke said with a note of petulance: "Well, why are you unburdening your soul to me? Aren't you afraid I'll report you?"

"No, I trust you. Basically you're just not the Titan type. I wanted you to know why I'm leaving. When things get bad – which they may – I want you to understand that *there is an alternative,* that Titan thinking isn't the only option for our species."

He raised his glass as though offering Heshke a toast. "To the future."

"Where will you go?" Heshke asked idly.

"In hiding for a bit. I have friends." Oblomot drained his glass. "Sorry to make a 'race traitor' of you, old man."

"That's all right," mumbled Heshke, waving his hand in embarrassment. "You know I could never bring myself to inform on you, Blare."

Lacking the energy to meet Oblomot's arguments, he left after a few more drinks and made his way to his own tent. It was night now; the full moon was out, casting a cold, eerie radiance over the ruins. He glanced up at the shining satellite, thinking briefly of the Titan outposts there, lonely sentinels guarding the approaches to Earth, watching the outskirts of the solar system for the return of the invader.

Then for the millionth time he turned his full attention to the ruins themselves. Even without moonlight there had always been something ghostly, unearthly, about them -- he couldn't quite put his finger on it, but he had always put it down to the fact that they were, after all, of alien origin. On the short stroll to his tent he placed his hand on a time-worn wall. It was chill – yet, in his imagination, the phrase *living rock* came to him. The stone did indeed seem to carry the ghost of life, as if redolent of the beings who had shaped it. He reminded himself of the inexplicable photographs and shook his head in despair. Towers and walls reconstructing themselves over the centuries. What incredible hoax had the faker tried to perpetrate?

In his tent, he went straight to bed, his conversation with Oblomot tumbling over and over in his mind. Yes, he told himself, the Titans *were* masters of propaganda. But the propaganda was about real things, not about the fake things – not like those photographs. Its strength lay in its appeal to a primeval urge of nature. *Blood and soil.* It was a rare man who could resist it.

And he, too, was of that blood, and of that soil.

He was awakened just before dawn by the whine of hoverjets.

Blearily he rose from his camp bed and peered through the tent flap to see two hoverjets bearing Titan insignia settle squarely in the middle of the camp. Two others remained in the air, standing off just outside the ruins.

It was a frankly military style of approach. The airborne helijets were in a guard posture, and carried glaring searchlights which cast the scene in vivid relief.

Hurriedly Heshke dressed and went outside. A traversing searchlight beam hit him full in the face, transfixed him for a moment or two, then moved on. When his vision returned to normal he saw that two Titan noncoms were striding towards him.

"Are you Citizen Heshke?" one demanded. He nodded.

19

"Come with us, please." They turned and strode off, leaving him to straggle after them.

The slim figure of Titan-Captain Brask stood by the nearer hoverjet. "Good morning, Heshke," he said in a supercilious but not unfriendly voice. "We did warn you to be ready. Unfortunately it seems we need you somewhat sooner than we thought we would."

Heshke said nothing, his brain still slow with sleep. "Is there anything you need to bring with you?" Brask asked politely. "Books, notes, charts? Well, we can supply anything you want, anyway."

He turned. Blare Oblomot was approaching, walking slowly between Titan escorts. In the background Heshke saw some of his helpers emerging from their tents to stare curiously, white figures in pre-dawn darkness.

"Is my assistant Oblomot included in this project too?" he queried.

Brask gave a short, sharp laugh. "Oh, we know all about him. He's got a different destination."

As he came near, Oblomot gave Heshke a half pleading, half I-told-you-so look. Brask made a violent gesture with his arm.

"Take him to Major Brourne at Bupolbloc Two. Heshke comes with us."

Heshke watched his friend being put aboard the second hoverjet, feeling sick inside. Bupolbloc Two, he thought. He hadn't known there was a Number Two; hadn't known that the building he had visited just yesterday was only Bupolbloc One.

Suddenly he reminded himself that his small personal belongings and toilet requisites were still in his tent, but he decided against returning to collect them. Brask looked impatient, and anyway the Titans were very efficient at providing details like that.

Numbly he climbed into the hoverjet. They surged upward and whined away to the north.

Suddenly there was a glare of light and the sound of an explosion from one of the other helijets, the one carrying Blare Oblomot. Heshke gasped with shock, and saw the flaring skeleton of the jet plummeting earthward in the darkness.

Brask jumped to his feet, cursing. "The fools! Didn't they know enough to check him? He must have been carrying a suicide grenade!"

Heshke tore his gaze away from the blaze on the ground and

20

gaped at him. Brask gave him a sidelong glance.

"You don't know about these, do you? The underground has been using that trick quite a lot lately. Saves them from interrogation and takes a few of us with them."

Unsuspected vistas seemed to be opening up to Heshke. "I . . . no, I hadn't known."

"Naturally, you wouldn't. It's not advertised on the media, and we have ways of discouraging rumour. Yes, there is an organised underground and your friend Oblomot was a member of it. You didn't know that either – or did you?" Brask's odd, quizzical gaze darted toward him.

"No, I hadn't known – not until tonight," Heshke murmured.

They hovered over the spot for a few minutes, watching the wrecked jet burn itself out. Finally one of the three remaining jets put down beside it. The other two continued the journey as the sun rose, whistling toward a destination that still had not been divulged to Heshke.

3.

At the city of Cymbel they transferred to a fast intercontinental rocket transport. On board Heshke was given breakfast, but Brask said little during the two-hour journey. Once he went forward to the guidance cabin to receive a radio message and returned looking pensive.

They had chased the twilight zone on their five thousand mile trajectory, so it was still early morning when they arrived at their destination. The rocket transport put down at what was evidently a private landing strip. A car drove up to take them to a low, massive concrete building a few hundred yards away.

Once inside the building Heshke found himself confronted with the usual Titan combination of efficiency and bustle. The corridors literally hummed – he didn't know from what source. Symbols whose meanings he did not understand signposted the way to various departments. He turned to Brask.

"What is this place?"

"A top secret research station."

"Is the artifact here?"

Brask nodded. "That's why this centre was set up – to study the artifact."

Heshke's eyebrows rose. "Then how long ago was it found?"

"Just over five years."

"Five *years*? And you've kept quiet about it all that time?"

Brask smiled distantly. "Patience, Citizen. You'll understand everything shortly."

They came to a heavy door guarded by two armed Titans. Brask presented a pass; the door opened with the sigh of a pneumatic lock.

Beyond the guarded door the atmosphere was quieter and more calm. "This leads to the main research area," Brask told him. "I'll introduce you to your new colleagues shortly. They begin the day here with an ideological session – would you care to drop in on it? It must be nearly over now."

Resignedly Heshke nodded. Brask led him down a corridor and they entered a small auditorium. An audience of about two hundred white-smocked men and women faced a large screen which illustrated a commentary by means of a succession of pictures.

The visualisation, Heshke noted, was skilled and professional. The scene at the moment was a soulful one of the sun setting over the forest-clad hills; in the foreground a deep blue sea lapped against a rocky, encrusted shore.

But smoothly the picture merged into a slow collage of viruses and soil bacteria. The sudden transition from the expansive world of forest, sea and sun to the invisible, microscopic world at the boundary of life was, Heshke thought, effective. It caught his attention right away, and he listened with interest to the mature, persuasive voice that accompanied the vidtrack, knitting the brief scenes together into a coherent whole.

"Here we have the *germinal essence*," purred the voice on the audtrack. "In these primary particles of life the spirit and essence of the planet Earth has concentrated all its being. By means of a mighty distillation from the potentiality of rock and soil, sun, ocean and lightning, were created these seeds of all future things. From this moment Earth, which before was barren, has produced DNA; and from this DNA, like a giant rising from the sea, there inevitably springs in due season the culmination of the entire process: the entity for which all the rest of Terrestrial life is but a platform. This is known as the *culminating essence*, or the *human essence*."

The pictures that illustrated this speech were swift and dizzying. The virus forms vanished; momentary images of DNA helices, dancing chromosomes and dividing cell nuclei appeared one after the other, interspersed with a swift procession of diverse living species as the stages of evolution unfolded.

At the end of the sequence, to coincide with the speaker's last words, appeared the image of a young, naked male, godlike both in proportion and feature (and posed no doubt by a suitable Titan). The figure stood with arms outstretched, light streaming around his silhouette from a point source in the background, slowly fading into a picture of Earth swimming in space.

23

"It follows," continued the voice soberly, "that evolution is *not* a series of arbitrary accidents but a *whole process*, tending toward a predestined end. It follows that by nature Earth produces but *one* supreme species, this being her destiny, and it follows that this is a law holding for all planets throughout the universe. Earth is our mother, our home, our sustenance. From Earth's soil we draw our blood. We are her sons; no one shall take her from us."

With a sonorous orchestral chord the screen went blank. Heshke was fascinated. Blood and soil, he thought again. There was much in the lecture that, paradoxically, was both appealing and repellent: the mysticism, the blatant Earth-worship, the belief in destiny. But who knows, he thought, there might be something in it. Perhaps evolution *does* work like that.

The audience rose and filed out silently. Brask nudged Heshke. "Now you can meet the people you'll be working with."

Three members of the audience stayed behind, going over to a small table at the back. Brask and Heshke joined them.

Two of the men had the armbands and precise bearing of Titans. The third was a civilian, standing out from the others by reason of his sloppy slouch. He had a habit of glancing furtively around him, as if wishing he were somewhere else, and his mouth was twisted into a permanent expression of sardonic bitterness.

Brask made introductions. "Titan-Lieutenant Vardanian, Titan-Lieutenant Spawart, Citizen Leard Ascar. Gentlemen, this is Citizen Rond Heshke."

All made brief bows.

"Are you gentlemen archaeologists also?" Heshke asked as politely as he could, since he did not recognise their names.

"No, we are physicists," Leard Ascar said shortly. His voice matched his face, ironical, mocking.

Brask motioned them to chairs. "It's time to put you into the picture, Citizen," he said to Heshke. "I hope you're able to absorb strange facts at short notice, because you'll need to."

He flicked a switch on a small console on the table. The big screen lit up, but for the moment remained without a picture.

"We told you earlier that we had discovered an alien artifact in working order. You probably imagined it had been found in a dig or something of that sort. In point of fact it was discovered lying in the open on a grass field, quite accidentally, far from any known alien remains. Moreover it was obviously of very recent manufacture."

24

He flashed a picture on the screen. The background was as he had described: a grassy meadow, with a line of trees in the distance. Lying in the foreground was a silvery cylinder, rounded at both ends and with dull, rather opaque-looking windows set fore and aft. A Titan stood by it for size comparison, revealing it to be about seven feet in diameter and about twelve in length.

"As you see, it's a vehicle of some sort," Brask continued. "Within were two aliens who appeared to have died shortly before of asphyxiation. As these were our first complete specimens they have increased our knowledge of the enemy to quite an extent."

The screen blanked for a moment and then flicked to another picture. The cylinder had been opened. The two occupants, seen partially because of the awkwardness of handling the camera through the opening, were strapped side by side in narrow bucket seats. They were small furry creatures with pointed snouts and pink mole-like hands, being perhaps the size of young chimpanzees. After a few seconds the picture flickered and the same two corpses were shown more completely, pinned to a slab in a Titan laboratory.

Despite his excitement, Heshke found time to be pleased that the specimens resembled quite closely the reconstructions that had been attempted from skeletons.

"So it was a spaceship," he said.

"That was naturally our conclusion, to begin with. But we were wrong. Only gradually, by experimenting with the vehicle's drive unit, were we able to piece together what it did."

Heshke noticed that the physicists were all looking at the floor, as though hearing the subject talked about embarrassed them.

"The equipment aboard the vessel used a principle completely unknown to us," Brask went on. "Movement through space – through comparatively short distances of space, not interplanetary space – could in fact be achieved as a by-product, but that was not its main purpose. Its main purpose is to move through time. The artifact we had stumbled on was a time machine."

The physicists continued looking at the floor. Heshke let the bombshell sink into his mind.

Time. A time machine. The archaeologist's dream.

"So they're from the past," he said finally, staring at the picture of the alien time travellers.

Brask nodded. "That would be the assumption. Presumably they developed the means of time travel during the final stages

25

of their sojourn on Earth, but too late to do them any good. We can only hope the secret is not known on their home world, but frankly I think we would have felt some effect from it if it was."

"Yes, indeed," Heshke muttered. "The whole thing is – frightening."

"You've said it," Brask responded.

Heshke coughed nervously. "This field trip I'm going on," he said after a pause. "It's a trip through time?"

"Perhaps. Perhaps not."

"I don't understand."

Brask looked at Titan-Lieutenant Vardanian. "Would you care to explain?"

The tall Titan physicist nodded and turned to Heshke.

"You'll appreciate that we had no intention of risking our only time machine in reckless jaunts. We've spent five years of hard work trying to grasp the operation of the time traveller so that we could duplicate it. Finally we completed our own operational traveller – so we thought – and have made some trips in it. But the results are such that we need your expert advice; we're no longer sure that our traveller works properly."

Heshke didn't understand what he meant. The Titan turned to the screen, reached for the control box and eliminated the image of the dead alien pilots. "Watch carefully. I'm going to show you some pictures our men took."

A flurry appeared on the screen, then an impression of racing motion as if some colourful scene were swinging wildly to and fro and passing by too swiftly to be grasped properly. After some moments Heshke discerned that the only stable element in the picture was a sort of rim on the upper and lower edges; he realised that this was the rim of another screen or window through which the camera was taking the sequence.

He found it hard to believe that all this was really happening. Here he was seeing pictures from the past while an efficient, intelligent Titan officer calmly explained something he would have thought to be impossible. It made even the death of Blare Oblomot seem a shadowy, dream-like event.

Suddenly the picture stilled. They looked out over an even landscape, the sun high in the sky. In the middle ground stood clumps of ruins stretching for several miles. Though so corroded and overgrown as nearly to have blended into nature, to Heshke's trained eye they clearly showed their alien origin.

"The Verichi Ruins, approximately nine hundred years ago," Vardanian said quietly. "Not what you would expect, is it?"

No, thought Heshke, it certainly wasn't. Nine centuries ago the Verichi Ruins – ruins in the present century, that is – should have been in their prime: an inhabited, bustling city. He watched an armoured figure stumbling about some heaps of stones. "It's more like what they'll be nine centuries in the future," he agreed. "Maybe you were headed in the wrong direction?"

"Our conclusion also, at first," Vardanian told him. "Initially we made five stops, all inside a bracket covering two centuries. We failed to find any living aliens at all, merely ruins such as you see here. However, it didn't take long to ascertain that the wars of collapse – the death-throes of classical civilisation – *were* in progress simultaneously with the existence of these ruins. So we *were* in the past after all."

"But that doesn't make sense," Heshke objected, frowning.

"Agreed. According to everything we know there *was* a large alien presence at the time of the wars of collapse. Could we be wrong? Could the alien presence have been much earlier? That would explain the dilapidated condition of the ruins – but it would *not* explain their much fresher condition today. Frankly, none of the historical explanations make much sense. So we were forced to draw other, more disappointing conclusions: that the time traveller was playing tricks on us, that we weren't travelling through time at all."

"You're beginning to lose me. Where *were* you going?"

Vardanian gestured vaguely, as though searching for words to express thoughts he only understood as abstract symbols. "There are some peculiarities about the time-drive that suggest other possibilities. In order to work at all it has to be in the presence of a wakened consciousness; an unmanned, automatic time traveller simply wouldn't move. So a living pilot is one of the essential components. Bearing this in mind, we were able to formulate a theory that the traveller – the one we have built, at any rate, even if not the alien one – fails to move through *objective* time. It enters some region of 'fictitious time', and presents to the consciousness of the observer elements from both the past and the future blended together, probably drawing them from the subconscious imaginations of the pilot and passengers."

"It's all an illusion, you mean?"

The other nodded doubtfully. "Roughly speaking, yes. Though

the time traveller obviously does go *somewhere*, because it disappears from the laboratory."

Heshke noticed that throughout the latter part of this explanation Leard Ascar scowled and muttered under his breath. Vardanian glanced at him pointedly. "That, with one dissenting vote, was the explanation we had adopted until yesterday."

"And then you showed us those photographs," Brask put in. "That upset things somewhat."

Yes, the photographs. The pictures that showed the Hathar Ruins three centuries ago, and showed them in worse condition than they are today. The pictures that obviously – perfectly, clearly, obviously – were faked. The pictures that could not possibly be true.

"It was too much of a coincidence," Brask said. "Here was independent, objective evidence of the findings that *we* had thought were subjective and illusory. We immediately dispatched the time traveller to Hathar at around the time these photographs were presumably taken, and took a corresponding set of photographs from the same viewpoints." He opened a drawer underneath the table and withdrew a sheaf of glossy prints. "Here are copies of both sets. Check them: you'll find they match, more or less."

Heshke did as he was told, looking over the prints. One set was in colour, the other – the old ones – in monochrome. He pushed them away, feeling that he was being surrounded by too much strangeness for one day.

"Yes, they look similar. What does that prove? That you *did* travel back in time after all?"

"Yes," said Leard Ascar fiercely, speaking for the first time.

And the other Titan, Spawart, also spoke for the first time. He adopted an expression of meticulous care, choosing his words slowly. "It may not necessarily mean that. We can't really take these photographs as substantiating our own findings. They *could* have been faked. Or, knowing now that time travel is possible, they *could* have been displaced in time, owing their origin to our future. There are a number of possibilities which do not rule out a malfunction in our time traveller."

Yes, thought Heshke. Someone sent a package of photographs from three hundred years in the future to three hundred years in the past – a hop of six hundred years. That could have happened. But why?

It was useless to speculate. There could be a thousand bizarre,

28

trivial, or unguessable reasons.

"Gentlemen," he said, "I'm finding this all just a little bit too bewildering. Do you mind telling me exactly why I'm here?"

"Yes, of course," said Brask solicitously. "We hadn't meant to call on your services until we had ironed the defects out of our time-drive system, but these photographs have thrown us somewhat into confusion. So we want you to take a trip back to the Hathar Ruins of three hundred years ago."

"Why?" Heshke asked.

"Well —" Brask hesitated. "We're working in the dark at the moment. Our most pressing need is to know whether our present capacity to travel through time is objectively real or merely illusory. The psychologists tell us that if it *is* illusory then there will be anomalies in the structures that appear to exist outside our own time – much as a dream fails to reconstruct reality with accuracy. There would be something to distinguish the ruins in the second set of photographs from the *real* Hathar Ruins."

Heshke glanced again at the two sets. "They don't look much different to me."

"Agreed. But perhaps there's a difference the pictures don't show. Now you know the Hathar Ruins better than anyone: they're your speciality. We just want you to go back and make a study of them; see if you can throw any light on the mystery."

"Those are pretty vague directives."

Brask shrugged. "Quite so. But Leard will be going with you; perhaps you can work something out together."

Heshke contemplated for a few moments. "This travel into a 'fictitious past': it would be like a descent into the subconscious mind, wouldn't it?"

"Possibly so," Titan-Lieutenant Vardanian said. But Leard Ascar gave vent to a derisive guffaw.

"Take no notice of all this nonsense, Heshke," he said waspishly. " 'Fictitious past,' my eye! The time-drive works!"

"Then the ruins . . . ?" Heshke inquired delicately.

Ascar shrugged and then seemed to retreat into himself.

Heshke turned to Brask. "When do we go?"

"As soon as possible. If you feel up to it, today."

"I'll need recorders, and a few tools."

The other nodded. "We've anticipated that. I think you'll find we have everything you could require."

"You mentioned danger. . . ."

29

"Only because the unit is relatively untested. That's the only source of risk."

"Apart from other aliens?" Heshke queried. "This business makes their technology look pretty formidable."

"Yes, but not necessarily in all-area advance of our own," Spawart replied. "After all, we were able to copy their time-drive. That would indicate that we have comparable ability."

"That is, provided we *have* copied it," Brask rejoindered, giving the other a sharp look.

"Of course we have!" snapped Ascar.

Heshke first inspected his equipment, and then was given a private room in which to rest. He slept for a couple of hours and then lay on the couch thinking over everything he had learned.

The expedition, he gathered, was to comprise four men in all: himself, the physicist Leard Ascar, and two Titan technical officers to pilot the time traveller. Departure was timed for midafternoon, and as the day wore on his nerves began to fray.

Shortly after lunch had been brought to him he was visited by Leard Ascar, who had spent the morning working on the time apparatus.

"Hello, Heshke, feeling nervous?" the sour-faced physicist said.

Heshke nodded.

"No need to worry. It's all quite safe and painless really. This is my third trip."

"How long will the journey take?"

"We can manage a hundred years per hour. So say three hours there, three hours back."

"We're rather a long way from Hathar, aren't we – in spatial terms, I mean?"

"No problem. While we're travelling through time – strictly speaking we're travelling through *non*-time – we can manoeuvre over the Earth's surface at will. We'll land slap on top of our target."

"From here to Hathar in three hours," Heshke mused. "That's not bad at all. This time machine would make quite a good intercontinental transport, then?"

Ascar laughed shortly. "You're quick on the uptake, but no, it wouldn't. You have to trade space for time. To travel to the other side of the Earth you'd have to traverse about a hundred years. I suppose you could do it by moving back and forth until you matched destinations in space *and* time, but after you'd finished messing about you would have done better to go by rocket."

Ascar fumbled in his pocket, brought out a crumpled tobacco roll and lit it, breathing aromatic smoke all around. Heshke noticed that his eyes bulged slightly. "Mind if I sit down? Been working on that damned time-drive all morning. I'm kind of tensed up myself."

"Sure, be my guest." Ascar took the room's only chair and Heshke sat on his bed to face him. "I'm rather curious . . . how does the time traveller work?"

Ascar grinned. "By detaching 'now' from 'now' and moving it through 'non-now'.

Heshke shook his head with a sigh. "That means absolutely nothing to me."

"It wouldn't have to me, either, before we found the alien machine. And not even then for a long time. But I understand it now. That's why I'm sure the Titans are wrong with this cockeyed notion of 'subconscious time' or whatever." Ascar puffed on his roll as if tobacco were the staff of life. Heshke realised that the man was even more nervous than he was. "I'm sorry, Heshke, it's just that I think this whole jaunt is a waste of time. The time traveller does what we intended it to do: to travel, objectively and in reality, back and forward through time. And I'm the one to ask because it was *me*, in the end, who cracked the problem. *They'd* still be fumbling."

"What's this, professional jealousy?" Heshke smiled.

The other waved his hand and looked annoyed. "Why should I be jealous? The Titan scientists are good at their work – on straightforward problems. Give them a premise and they'll take it right through to its conclusion, very thoroughly. But where creative thinking is called for they tend to fall back on their ideology – and we all know what a lot of bull that is."

Heshke looked around uneasily, wondering about hidden microphones. "I never thought I'd hear anyone talk like that in a Titan stronghold," he said.

The physicist shrugged. "They tolerate me. I've been with this project from the start, five years ago. Things were more easygoing in the old days. I'm sick of it now, though."

"Oh? Why?"

Ascar sneered. "I've built them their time traveller and they say

31

it doesn't work, just because they don't like what they've discovered in the past. They're disappointed that the aliens didn't seem to have played any part in the wars of collapse, that's what it all comes down to. And we've hardly even done any exploring yet. Maybe the aliens *were* around, somewhere or other."

"You sound bitter."

Ascar pulled on his roll. "Just tired. Five years spent trying to understand time has unhinged my mind. Take no notice of my grumbling, Citizen. It's all part of my personality syndrome."

"But the ruins," Heshke reminded him. "If we were to take the evidence at face value they are growing *newer* as time passes, instead of older. That just can't be, can it?"

Ascar shrugged. "How the hell would I know? Nothing looks impossible to me now I know that time's mutable, that the individual's 'now' can be detached from absolute 'now'. There must be an explanation." He smiled. "How about this? Thousands of years ago the aliens flew over here and planted some seeds — special kinds of seeds. Ever since they've been slowly growing, not into plants or vegetable matter but into structures of stone and metal. The ruins we see are like trees maturing over centuries into full-blown houses, cities, castles and whatever. When they are fully grown the aliens will come down and live in them."

Heshke laughed, thinking over the idea. He was tickled by Ascar's quick imagination, by his readiness to face impossible facts and draw daring inferences from them. "But there are skeletons, too," he reminded. "The seeds wouldn't grow those."

"Why not? Maybe a few skeletons were included to fool future archaeologists." But Heshke could see that the physicist wasn't being serious.

There was silence for a while. Ascar smoked noisily and shuffled his feet, staring at the ceiling. He seemed to have become unaware of Heshke's presence.

"Has any attempt been made to contact people in the past?" Heshke asked then. "Probably they could answer a good many of our questions."

"Huh?" Ascar's attention jerked back into the room. He stared at Heshke with glazed eyes. "Oh. Oh, you don't know about that, do you?"

"Don't know about what?" asked Heshke in some exasperation.

"About what it's like in the past. You can't talk to the people there because they don't hear you. They don't see you, either.

What's more you can knock them down and they don't react in any way at all, just lie there squirming and eventually get up again. It's as if they were robots going through motions which time has already ordained."

Heshke stared at him.

"Oh, I know it sounds weird," Ascar said with a wave of his hand, "but that's how it is."

"Do you mean they have no consciousness?"

"They act like they have no consciousness. Like robots, pre-determined mechanisms," Ascar repeated.

"That sounds . . . sort of dream-like. Are you sure the Titans couldn't be right?"

"Oh no, it accords with my theory of how the time traveller works very well. You've probably read fictional stories about time travel and got your ideas of time from them. They always make the past or the future sound no different in essence from present time; but we know now that they're very different indeed."

The physicist finished his tobacco roll and threw away the end, groping in his pocket for another. Heshke gave him one and helped him light it. "How?"

"I'll explain. Think of the universe as a four-dimensional con-tinuum – three dimensions of space, as is our ordinary experience, and an additional dimension which we call time, extending into the infinite past and the infinite future. If we take the moving 'now' out of the picture we could just as easily call it a universe of four dimensions of space. So now we have a static four-dimensional matrix. That's basically what the universe consists of, but there's one other factor: the fleeting present moment, sweeping through the fourth dimension like a travelling wave."

Heshke was no physicist but he had read widely and to some extent was already familiar with what Ascar was saying. He nodded, picturing it to himself. "The 'now' that we seem to be trapped in, being moved on from one moment to the next."

"That's right. What is this 'now'? Does anything exist outside it? For centuries the philosophical question has been whether the past and the future have any existence, or whether only the present that we experience has existence. Well, we've found out the answer to that question all right: the past and the future *do* exist, but they have no 'now'. In effect, they have no time. No differentiation between before and after. They're both dead, as it were."

"So that's why the people in the past act like robots?"

Ascar nodded. "The travelling 'now-wave' has passed them by. Consciousness can only exist in the 'now' – somehow or other it appears to be a function of it."

"This time-wave – what does it consist of?"

"We're not really sure. Some form of energy that travels through the four-dimensional continuum like a shock wave. We know its velocity: it travels with the speed of light. And as it goes it has the power to make events happen and to organise matter into living forms. You know in olden times they used to talk about the 'life force'? This is the life force."

A thought occurred to Heshke. "You say there's no time in the past. But what if you went back in time and changed something? What happens to the past as it was *before* you changed it? There'd have to be a kind of time there because there'd be a *before* you changed it and an *after* you changed it. . . ." He broke off in confusion.

The physicist grinned. "What you're talking about used to be called the Regression Problem, and it exercised us too when we first realised time travel was possible. Actually, in a slightly different form, it's an ancient philosophical riddle: how can time pass without having another 'time' to pass in? One instant 'now' is at one point and the next instant it's at the adjacent point, passed on to the next event, and so you seem to have a 'before' and an 'after' associated with the same moment – one where 'now' was there and one where it wasn't."

"Yes, I think that's what I mean," Heshke said slowly.

Ascar nodded. "These paradoxes have largely disappeared now that we're able to make on-the-spot observations. Theorists used to posit an additional fifth dimension to accommodate these changes, but we know better than that now. The universe is indifferent to all artificially imposed changes, as well as to where 'now' is situated. It doesn't distinguish between one configuration and another: therefore any changes you make don't alter anything."

Heshke didn't understand him. "But there's still the old riddle, what if I went back and murdered my father before I was born . . . ?"

"It would probably turn out that your father was somebody else," Ascar said acidly. "Joking apart, if you did succeed in 'killing' your father, you'd find that he was still alive . . . later.

34

Cause and effect, as we understand it, only takes place in the travelling now-wave – what we call the Absolute Present. We've established that experimentally. Elsewhere the universe behaves indifferently, and if you *do* force changes on the past, then the consequences die away instead of accumulating."

"You're beginning to lose me," Heshke said slowly. "I find it hard to grasp . . . that even when tomorrow comes I shall still be here today, smoking this roll . . . only I won't be aware of it."

Ascar rubbed his jaw and yawned tiredly. "That's it: you've got it exactly. Now we are here; shortly the Absolute Present will have moved a few minutes further on, taking our consciousness with it. But the past doesn't vanish, it's merely that you can't see it – just as you can't see the future yet, even though it exists up there ahead of us. The time traveller acts like a lever, detaching a fragment of the present and moving it about independently. If that fragment has your consciousness attached to it you can then see the past, or the future."

"How far have you been into the future?" asked Heshke suddenly.

Again Ascar looked sour. "Only about a hundred years, no further. There's no point."

"Oh? Why not?"

"Because do you know what you find in the future? Just an empty desolation! There are no living forms – no people, no animals, no grass, no birds or trees or anything. Not a virus or a microbe. Just one second futureward of where we're sitting the world is void of all life, and these chairs we're sitting on are empty."

Horrified, Heshke blinked at him. Ascar smiled crookedly. "It's logical, if you think about it. There's life in the past, even if it does behave like clockwork, because the now-wave has already swept over it and the now-wave creates life. But it hasn't reached the future yet. Everything we've constructed out of inorganic matter – our buildings, our machines, and so on – are there, but without the hand of man to maintain them they fall into a state of decay. And as for the substance of our own bodies, that's dust, just dust."

And Heshke sat contemplating that vast, dead emptiness.

35

4.

The Titan time traveller was considerably larger than its alien prototype. Instead of the latter's cylindrical form it had a cage-like structure, being square at both ends and ribbed with louvres. One end contained the cabin for the crew and passengers, the other the bulky drive machinery. It did, however, borrow some features from the alien design: the windows were of a thick nearly-opaque material possessing the quality of image-control, capable of being adjusted so as to admit or block light, and the control system copied the alien concept in its entirety.

Initially the machine's departure from the present was assisted by a second, even larger apparatus from whose maw it currently projected like a tongue, but once dispatched it flew under its own power and had no contact with the home base. This fact was nagging at Heshke's consciousness as he tried to fight down his fears and allowed himself to be helped into the stiff combat armour the Titans had insisted he wear.

"Are you comfortable?" the young com-tech asked.

He nodded, though he was far from comfortable since the leather-like suit restricted all his movements.

For some minutes the Dispatch Room had been filled with a loud whine as the launcher was warmed up. Ascar was already in his suit, as were the two technical officers who were to pilot the time traveller. Ascar beckoned him forward.

"All set? Your gear all ready?"

"It's on board." Not that he anticipated using much; he didn't really know what he would do when he reached the ruins.

"Then let's take our places."

He followed Ascar into the time traveller. The cabin was comparatively large, about nine feet by nine. He sat down beside the physicist, strapping himself in. The tech officers came in, wearing their combat suits with more grace and style, and settled into the pilots' seats in the front of the cabin. The whine from the Dispatch Room was cut off as the door slid shut: the time traveller was soundproof.

Heshke's muscles knotted up. The tech officers murmured to one another and through microphones to the team outside. A raw, fuzzy hum arose to their rear.

One of the Titans half turned his head to speak to them. "We're away."

Was that all? Heshke's stomach untensed itself. He felt no sensation of motion; but through the semi-opaque windows he saw a runny blur of motion and colour, phasing wildly to and fro as though the vehicle were pursuing an erratic course.

"Home," Ascar said to him. "We're leaving home."

Heshke looked at him quizzically.

"Well of course it's home!" the other scowled impatiently. "Don't you know what I mean? Haven't you any vision?"

"I guess not."

"I mean we're leaving the Absolute Present. That's home to us. The only place in the universe where conscious life exists. Just think of all of past time, stretching back and back into eternity. The further back you go into it the further away you are from the brief intersection where life exists, until you would be like a ghost, a brief fragment of time in a timeless abyss . . . and the same if you go into the future. Doesn't that get through to you?"

Ascar's eyes were bulging and there were tiny beads of perspiration on his brow. "Is that what going back in time is like for you?" Heshke asked quietly. "Like falling into an abyss?"

"That's what it's like – a chasm without a bottom. And we're descending into it."

Suddenly Heshke understood Ascar. The man was afraid, for all that he had reassured Heshke. He was afraid that something would go wrong and they would be cut off, unable to get back to the world of life and time.

He had too vivid an imagination; and he was getting a little melodramatic. Heshke wondered if the physicist's five-year-long obsession had left him mentally unbalanced. After all, it was an awesome subject to have preying on one's mind.

Heshke himself still found the explanations of time and non-time too abstruse to be grasped properly; his mind spun when he tried to think it through. He found it hard to understand why the travelling wave of 'now', that is, of time, should be at one particular place at one particular *time*. . . .

No, that wasn't it, either. Being where it was was what *made* time. . . .

They passed the rest of the journey in silence, Ascar slouching in his chair, insofar as the combat suit would let him, and occasionally muttering to himself. Three hours passed; and then the tech officer warned them that they were coming in to land.

A gong sounded. The blurred, racing images that had almost lulled Heshke to sleep ceased, but he couldn't see anything definite through the thickened windows.

Ascar released his safety strap and invited Heshke to do the same. "Come and have a look out of the window," he said, "you might like to see this."

Heshke followed him and peered through one of the frosty windows. Ascar turned a knob and the plate cleared.

Outside was a scene reassuringly pleasant and familiar. Judging by the position of the sun it was midafternoon. Beneath a blue sky stretched greenery: a savannah interspersed with scrawny trees. And nearby, recognisable to Heshke despite the intervening three centuries, were the Hathar Ruins, broken, crumbled and moss-covered.

"Notice anything?" Ascar said expectantly.

And Heshke did notice something. A raven was flying across their field of view – or rather, it was not flying. Close enough for every feather of its outspread wings to stand out distinctly, it was hanging in midair, frozen and motionless.

"It's not moving," he murmured in wonderment.

"That's right." Ascar seemed secretly gleeful. "We're at a dead stop. Halted on one frozen instant."

A thought occurred suddenly to Heshke "But if that were so we wouldn't be able to see anything. Light would be frozen, too."

Ascar gave a superior smile. "A clever inference, Citizen, but a wrong one. There's no such thing as frozen light – its velocity is constant for *all* observers, which is the same as saying it's not properly a velocity at all. Few laymen understand that."

He gave a signal to the pilot. "Just the same, for practical purposes we need to explore an environment with all the features of our own, that is to say one that moves."

The pilot did something on the control panel. The raven bolted into action, flapped its wings and flew away. The savannah stirred in the breeze.

"Now we are travelling futureward at the rate of one second per second: the normal rate of time we are used to. This rate will persist automatically. We can go outside now."

The door hissed open, allowing fresh air into the cabin. Heshke moved to the rear of the cabin, picked up a movie vidcamera, a satchel of tools and a specimen bag. Then he followed Ascar into the open air.

There could be little doubt of it. The photographs dug up in Jejos weren't faked; there was no coincidence, nothing that could account for them in accidental terms. They were pictures of the actual ruins he and Ascar stood in the midst of now.

Beyond them, on a grassy knoll, stood the time traveller, guarded by one of the Titan technical officers. The other officer had taken up a nearer position just outside the ruins and was scanning the landscape for signs of danger. God knew what kind of danger there could be here in the middle of nowhere, three hundred years back in limbo, but there he stood in the textbook standoff position.

It was hard to believe it: hard to believe that they *were* three hundred years into non-time. The air brought to Heshke's nostrils all the freshness of summer, the sun shone down, and everything looked peacefully normal.

"Are you absolutely sure?" Ascar asked.

"Absolutely. I know these ruins like the back of my hand. I've been studying them for years. These *are* the Hathar Ruins, as I would expect them to be three centuries *after* our time. We *must* be in the future."

"No, we're in the past." Ascar was frowning, a scowling frown of great agitation.

"Well. . . ." Heshke put his hand on a weathered alien wall, feeling the almost subconscious thrill he had noted so often. "Then we're up against a paradox that would seem to support the Titan theory: that the past and the future have got mixed up somehow and nothing we see is real. But I have to say that personally I feel forced to reject even that theory. These remains are too perfect, too solid and incontrovertible in every detail. They *have* suffered three centuries of physical decay from the ruins of my time, and they have decayed exactly as I would expect."

"But we *are* in the past," Ascar insisted.

Heshke shouldered his vidcamera and shook his head sadly. "Come over here," he invited.

Clambering over the massy stones, the physicist followed him into a grid-pattern of low walls which had the appearance of once having been a set of rooms. The archaeologist crouched down beside a wall where he had earlier pulled away a patch of moss.

"This clinches it," he said, looking up at Ascar. "See these grooves?"

Ascar stooped. The sharp sunlight glinted on little fronds of moss, on dirt and sparkling stone, and made shadows in a number of short trenches cut in three blocks of stone, surrounding a third.

"Yes."

"I myself helped to cut those grooves. We suspected there was an aumbry behind here – a cupboard cut in the wall. And we were right. Afterwards we replaced the sealing stone. Here, give me a hand."

He took a couple of jemmies out of his tool satchel. Ascar helped him to lever away the slab. It came after a little effort, being not as thick or as solidly entrenched as it looked. Heshke shone a little light into the cavity thus revealed and moved aside so that Ascar could look.

"I'll bet a year's pay there's some writing in there. See if you can find it."

Ascar poked his head into the entrance. The recess was larger than its door suggested and smelled damp, but it was free of dust. On the opposite wall were some large letters, neatly cut with a powered stone inscriber.

"Skeleton thirty-one," he read slowly. "Glass vessel four hundred eighty-nine."

Heshke chuckled. "That's right. I inscribed that message myself. It was to record what we had found in there and their catalogue numbers."

Ascar stood up and took a deep breath.

"Well, there's your proof," Heshke told him. "Right now we are standing *after* our time, *not* before."

"Well, you're the expert," Ascar said amiably. "I can't argue with that."

The time traveller surged forward, and Heshke relaxed, idly watching the flurry of shapes and colours through the windows and listening to the fuzzy hum of the time-drive. For the first part of the journey back to the research centre he had tried to talk to Leard Ascar; but the physicist had retreated into himself and now sat staring with glazed eyes at the floor, either stupefied or engaged in deep meditation.

He had asked the pilots that he be allowed to release the safety straps, since they appeared to be superfluous and made the journey even more tedious, but they had refused, explaining that the machine was liable to a sudden lurch if a rapid change in direction was called for.

He wondered how his report would be received by the Titan controllers of the research centre. Already he had communicated his findings to the pilots. They were well-trained and understood the implications. But with typical Titan superciliousness they'd made no comment.

Half resentfully, he stared at their broad, uniformed backs. These Titans had killed his friend Blare Oblomot, he reminded himself. He realised now that he had gone around anaesthetised since that event, as if in a dream . . . it was a happening he just hadn't been able to take in properly. But then Blare, by his own admission, had been a traitor; inexplicably, a traitor. . . .

A gong rang out, in a different tone from that which had heralded the approach of their outgoing destination. The pilot spoke up for the passengers' benefit.

"We're approaching Absolute Present."

Ascar jerked his gaze up from the floor. Just then the co-pilot murmured something to his colleague, who glanced down at the other's section of the instrument panel.

"Citizen Ascar, we appear to have a malfunction on the Absolute Present register," the pilot announced in a puzzled tone.

"Eh?" Ascar released himself from his straps and bounded forward to peer closely at the designated instrument. From where he was sitting Heshke could see it: a large strip-dial that had commenced to flash as the gong sounded. A marker moved steadily across it in a count-down toward zero: the travelling wave of time.

But now the marker was quivering and behaving erratically, first darting toward the zero and then retreating from it. "Without that register we'll find it difficult to synchronise back into 'now'," the pilot warned.

"Malfunctioning, hell, it *must* be in order," Ascar growled.

"It gives impossible readings," the Titan corrected meticulously.

41

"It's obviously an instrument failure."

Ascar froze for a moment. "Not impossible," he said slowly. "It's detecting the presence of real time, but not strongly enough for it to be absolute time. Hell, we ourselves carry a small fragment of time with us – *as does every other time traveller!*"

He stepped to a window and tuned it to near-transparency, peered through it briefly and then crossed the cabin to do the same on the other side. There, pacing them so as to stand out steadily against the kaleidoscope-like flurry, was a cylindrical shape rounded at both ends.

It duplicated perfectly the alien time traveller that had been shown to Heshke on film.

Cautiously he released his straps and joined Ascar at the window, peering fascinated through the glowing pane. He became aware that behind the dulled windows of the alien traveller there were undoubtedly eyes, alien eyes, that were watching them.

"Great Mother Earth!" one of the Titans swore softly.

Ascar swung around. "For God's sake man – don't let them track us to the Research Centre!"

The Titan understood him perfectly. "Back to your seats!" he ordered. But Heshke was still not secured properly when the traveller gave a sickening lurch and raced off into whatever other direction might conceivably exist – Heshke was confused on that point for the moment. He just saved himself from being toppled onto the floor and fastened the straps.

The Absolute Present register was flaring more brightly. "We shall synchronise with the present on a distant part of Earth, and make our way from there to the Centre by conventional means," the Titan announced. "By that means we may hope to evade alien detection."

"No," said Ascar. "Keep going."

"What for?" the other said sharply. "Our orders are to return to the Centre forthwith!"

"Keep going – on into the future." Ascar's voice was trembling with excitement. "There's something I have to find out," he said. "Something we *all* have to find out. So keep going!"

The pilot glanced over his shoulder, perturbed – as Heshke was – to see the physicist so in the grip of passion. "Are you suggesting that we depart from the flight plan, Citizen? That can *not* be allowed! Any suggestions you may have will have to be put before the controllers."

"Yes, Titan ideologues who can't see the facts even when they're held up in front of their faces!" Ascar snarled, apparently in fury. "They'll delay, delay, delay – by then it might be too late! Mankind will be finished!"

Ascar had again stood up. Heshke was alarmed to see that he had produced a gun from somewhere in his combat suit. With a cry Heshke also scrambled free of his straps and staggered forward, recklessly intending to tackle him. But at that moment Ascar lunged, seizing a handgrip on the control panel and swinging it far over. The time traveller accelerated wildly and overshot the Absolute Present to hurtle wildly futureward. The accompanying jolt sent Heshke reeling. He fell, hit his head violently against the arm of a chair, and blackness overwhelmed him.

He came round to find himself back in his seat, lolling against the straps. His head ached abominably. But the pain was soon forgotten in the horror and shock of what he saw.

The co-pilot was lying against one wall, evidently dead. The other Titan was disarmed and stood against the opposite wall, warily watching Ascar who was nonchalantly piloting the time traveller while keeping an eye on him.

"Uh – what happened?" Heshke rasped.

Ascar spared him a glance. "Welcome back. I'm afraid there was a scuffle. Lieutenant Hosk got shot. Wasn't really my fault." He spoke the last in a surly mumble

Heshke paused. "And the alien time traveller?"

"We lost it." Ascar gave a tight, sinister grin. "I've been pushing this ship to its limit – close to a hundred and fifty years per hour."

The words "You're mad" died in Heshke's throat.

"Where are we now?"

"Nearly four hundred years in the future."

Heshke lay back in his seat, trying to fight off a feeling of hopelessness. Ascar's mind had evidently snapped under the strain. He and the pilot would have to be patient and await their chance to overwhelm him.

"The future? What do you expect to find there?" he asked, stumbling over the words. "You said yourself it's all dead and empty."

"The facts are staring us in the face," Ascar replied. "That's the mark of the true scientist, isn't it, Heshke? To take facts as

43

facts even if they conflict with theory, and draw the most obvious deductions from them. That's what we've been failing to do."

"What facts are those?" Heshke glanced nervously at the Titan, who was watching Ascar warily.

"Chiefly, the plain fact that the alien interventionist ruins are *ageing backward in time*. If we take that at face value, then their source lies in the future, and we're going to track it down."

His words were interrupted by the sounding of the gong. The Absolute Present register began to glow, for the second time this trip.

"There she blows!" crowed Ascar.

The Titan's jaw dropped. He stared at the register as though unable to believe his eyes.

"But we're four centuries away from Absolute Present!"

"Four centuries from *our* Absolute Present."

"There *is* only one," the Titan insisted emptily. "Your own equations say so . . . you to whom we owe the secret of the time-drive . . ."

"Well, I can't be right all the time," Ascar said, rather bleakly. "What do you think I was doing for three hours while we made the journey back – just sitting there with a blank mind?" He snorted. "Oh no, I was going over those very equations you seem to regard as sacrosanct . . . and it occurred to me that I might not know as much about time as I had thought, and that the equations could be wrong. So I began to imagine a number of other possibilities. What if the Absolute Present *isn't* unique, as I had formerly assumed it to be? Perhaps there are other waves of time, separated from our own by millions of years, by millennia – or only by centuries. Perhaps there is a regular series of them, forming the nodes of a cosmic wave frequency vibrating through the universe. Whatever the truth, I discovered that if I amended the equations to make room for any of these possibilities then the basic principle that makes the time-drive work remains unchanged . . . so the theoretical structure had to give way . . . even if the Great Earth Mother has to give way too. . . ."

While he spoke Ascar had been deftly flying the time traveller, dividing his attention between the instruments and his two hijacked passengers. His gun was never more than an inch or two away from his right hand.

He continued ramblingly. "And what if one of those other time waves was travelling *in the opposite direction* to our own? Not

44

proceeding from the past into the future, as we understand time, but from the future into the past? The very words past and future tend to lose their meaning in such a context. . . . Whatever lies behind one's direction of motion is the past and whatever lies in front of it is the future. . . . *There it is!"*

His last words were a shout, an excited squawk. The Absolute Present register had zeroed in and stood slightly on the other side of zero.

Ascar turned a knob, tuning the windows to transparency. "Take a look," he said. "We're at time-stop."

Slowly Heshke rose and approached one of the windows.

It was Earth, but it was not Earth. The sky was blue, with white clouds hanging majestically in it. The sun was of a familiar size, colour and radiance. But there the resemblance ended. True, there was grass – green grass . . . but it was an olive green shot through with mother-of-pearl colours, and all the other vegetation was distinctly non-Terran; the trees – twisted, writhing things – bore no resemblance to any Earth tree that had ever existed as far as Heshke knew.

These trees, growing on the slope of a grassy eminence where Ascar had set them down, did not detain his attention for long. Briefly he noted an unrecognisable flying thing, frozen in midair as had been the raven, and then he flooded his vision with the incredible scene that was set out below.

The Hathar Ruins: but not the ruins that Heshke had studied for so many years, and not those still further back down the centuries. This was the Hathar site as it had been in its prime: an intact, inhabited settlement. He drank in the clean-cut, sparkling conical towers, the large buildings, the Cathedral (whose purpose he still did not know), the tenement-like masses of smaller rooms, the plazas, the roads. . . .

It was all as he had constructed it in his imagination so many times. Alien, but *alive*. A bustling, living habitation of a non-human people.

And those people thronged Hathar. Furry, sharp-snouted, standing in triangular doorways and walking the streets and squares. But they were caught in mid-motion like a stereo still photograph: the traveller was not moving in any direction in time.

"The alien interventionists!" breathed the Titan officer. Both he and Heshke had forgotten their tacit agreement to jump Ascar.

"Correct. But they are not interventionists, though they are alien in a sense."

The Titan clenched his fists. "So we have been mistaken all along. The enemy is attacking from the *future*. That must be where he made his landings on Earth."

"No, no," said Ascar, adopting a tone of uncharacteristic patience. "Watch this: I'm putting us in motion again at the biological rate of one second per second."

He made an adjustment. The scene came to life. The clouds sailed across the sky, the trees moved, the aliens walked through streets and squares.

"They're walking backward," said Heshke blankly.

And so indeed they were. The whole scene was like a motion picture thrown into reverse. "That's because we've adopted the time sense normal to us," Ascar explained, "but it's not normal to *them*. Now watch what happens when I put our machine into reverse at the same rate – one second per second."

Again he made an adjustment. They all watched through the windows while the scene rewound itself and went forward, the alien creatures walking naturally this time, with a rolling gait, their posture not quite as erect as that of a human being. "*This* is their normal time-sense," Ascar told them, "the reverse of ours. *Now* do you get it? These creatures aren't alien to Earth. They're Terran. They evolved here, millions of years in our future. By the same token, we are in *their* future. The Earth has two completely different evolutionary developments on it, separated in time and associated with separate time-streams – time-streams moving in opposite directions. *And they are on a collision course.*"

The shock that affected Heshke and the Lieutenant, once they understood this news, lasted some time. They stared for long moments without speaking.

"But the Earth Mother," the Titan stuttered.

Ascar gave a harsh laugh. "Earth Mother!" He made the words sound like a curse.

Heshke turned to Ascar and gestured with his thumb through the window. "Aren't we too exposed? What if they see us?"

"They can't see us. We're not synched on their present moment; we're pacing a few minutes behind it."

"Collision!" gasped the Titan. "It's inconceivable! What will happen, Ascar?"

Ascar laughed again, this time horribly and savagely. "Can't you envisage it? The converging time processes are now only four hundred years apart, and already we've become aware of one another. Each will make massive preparations to destroy the other." His eyes shone, as though he were privy to some dreadful vision. "And while the time-waves are yet centuries apart an indescribable war of annihilation will be in progress. Each civilisation, on seeing the constructions of the other rising magically in its midst, on seeing them become *newer* with each passing year, will grow more and more fearful. Both sides will find themselves trying to manipulate *the same materials* from different points in time! But everything will be in vain – for what will happen when the two time-streams actually collide? Can anything survive such a shock? Annihilation, that's what will happen. Annihilation, followed by the cessation of all time. . . ."

With an effort the Titan broke free from the spell of Ascar's words. He drew himself erect.

"There's no time to lose: the High Command must be made aware of the situation immediately."

"Yes, that's where our duty lies." Ascar was trembling with nervous reaction. He drew back from the pilot's seat, leaving his gun where it was, and wiped his brow with a shaky hand. "Take over, Lieutenant."

The Titan seated himself at the control panels and made calibrations. He appeared to have recovered his composure completely and spoke with authoritative self-righteousness.

"It has to be admitted that you've rendered mankind a service, Citizen Ascar. Nevertheless when we return to Absolute Present you will be charged with disobeying orders and with murdering a Titan officer."

"Leave him alone, for God's sake," Heshke pleaded worriedly. "Can't you see he's insane?"

"Yes, insane," muttered Ascar. "Who wouldn't be . . . five years alone in that place. Who wouldn't be? The strain . . . knowing I was the only man on Earth who could solve the problem . . . who could give humanity the secret of time travel . . . I wasn't sure I could do it. The enemy had an advantage over us. We had to take away that advantage or perish . . . now we're going to perish anyway."

The fuzzy hum of the time traveller rose in volume as the machine picked up power and glided away from its position to

47

go surging pastward. Heshke settled down for the journey, reassured by seeing the tall Titan once more at the controls and by Ascar's apparent lapse into inactivity.

For about an hour they journeyed in silence. Heshke began to doze, but was awakened by a hoarse cry from the pilot, accompanied by a sickening lurch. The pilot was taking evasive action.

Heshke observed that the Absolute Present register was again flickering. The pilot cleared the windows to transparency to reveal the shape of a pursuing enemy time machine. Ascar shouted incoherently; at the same time they sustained a shuddering shock and seemed to go into a kind of spin.

Heshke became dizzy. When his head cleared the cabin was motionless, but leaning crazily, and a large hole had been torn in its side. Behind them the drive-unit gave out a ragged, injured buzz.

Somehow it came as a surprise to Heshke to find that the alien time traveller had been armed.

"Damn!" moaned Ascar. "Damn!"

Heshke got to his feet. The Titan officer was already peering out of the smoking hole in the side of the cabin. Heshke joined him and saw, in midair, a cylindrical shape half materialise, shimmering, and then fade away again. He shrank back momentarily; then, when the officer stepped cautiously to the ground, he followed him and stood staring around.

If death was the absence of life, then Heshke had never imagined such an expanse of death. The landscape stretched all around them in a grey, sterile tableland, featureless except for some hills in the west and some tumbled ruins to the north. There was not a blade of grass nor anything that moved. And dust, everywhere dust – Heshke had never conceived of so much dust, unless it was on the surface of the moon.

Ascar scrambled out of the cabin after them, his face gone ghastly pale. "The drive's ruined!" he exclaimed in a strangled tone. "That bastard knew exactly where to aim for!"

His glance darted around helplessly. "You asked me about the future, Heshke – well, here it is. The future that time hasn't reached yet. And we're stranded in it!"

That was what he was afraid of, Heshke thought.

"We've failed," said the Lieutenant in a stricken voice. "Our comrades will never hear our report now."

"It doesn't matter, you fool," Ascar snarled. "Life on Earth has exactly two centuries to run – then *everything's* finished."

Blood and soil, Heshke thought. *Blood and soil.*

They all stood staring at the dead landscape.

5.

Far from earth, the ISS – Interstellar Space Society – known to its inhabitants as Retort City floated as if transfixed in the blackness of space, approximately mid-way between Altair and Barnard's Star – that is, as far from any celestial body as it could manage. It took its name from its appearance, which was that of a double retort, or hourglass, but long and elegantly shaped. Retort City was, in fact, a city in a bottle, its outer skin being transparent and having a glassy sheen. An observer watching from the void would have discerned within the glass envelope a sort of double spindle, this being the general plan of the city's internal structure, and would have seen through a muted blaze of lights an intermittent movement as the internal transport facilities passed up and down.

The city had a history of about five thousand years, having lived it uneventfully for the most part. Probably, its rulers thought, there were other ISS establishments somewhere within a hundred light-year radius of Sol, all surviving fragments of long-vanished Earth civilisations, for at one time the idea of forsaking life on planetary bodies and taking to artificial cities in the interstellar void had been a fashionable one. But they did not know this for sure, and felt no urge to comb space for their lost cousins.

Colloquially the two halves of the ISS were known as the Lower Retort and the Upper Retort – terms with social, rather than spatial implications. Officially they were the Production Retort and Leisure Retort. And no one, except newborn babes, ever passed from one retort to the other.

Or almost no one.

Hueh Su Mueng shut down his machine and stood for a few moments looking abstractedly around him at the work area: a large, spacious hall filled with rows of machines, some like his own,

50

some different. The next shift was already beginning to wander in; some of the men stood around chatting, others looked over their spec sheets or started up their machines, already becoming absorbed in their work.

Most of Su-Mueng's shift had already gone. He was about to follow them when a young man, a few years older than himself, stopped by with a smile.

"Hello, Su-Mueng. There's nothing much doing in my section today. Got anything you'd like me to be getting on with?"

Su-Mueng hesitated. He had been finding his current job interesting and had intended returning tomorrow to continue it – had, in fact, been postponing the final stage of his *other* project so as to be able to complete it. He glanced down at the half finished assembly of finely-machined components: a new type of calibrator for some unguessable instrument wanted in the Upper Retort.

"Oh, all right. You can carry on with this," he said resignedly. He pulled out the spec sheets and explained the details and where he'd got to. "There's no hurry," he added. "Deadline's more than a month away."

The other man nodded, looking eagerly over the work. "It's always like that on these slow cycles. I hate it when we're so slack."

Su-Mueng walked away and discarded his work-gown in the locker room, washing his hands and face and using a refresher spray on himself. The hormone-laden mist settled on his skin and in his nostrils, making him feel fresher and brighter and washing away the weariness that comes from long hours of effort.

Then he strode away and down spiral staircases to the elevators, a slim, elegant youth. His mind began to buzz with thoughts and the excitement of his secret rebellion . . . but in the elevator that sped towards his domestic level he encountered Li Kim, an old friend he knew from training school, who pressed him to enjoy a short game of ping-pong. Not being able to think of a good reason to refuse, Su-Mueng left the elevator with him and they proceeded together to the nearest recreation hall.

Kim invoked two cans of beer from a dispenser and handed Su-Mueng one. They strolled through a gallery of gaming machines, then past the entrances to the theatres. Further on there was a thumping noise against the wall from some fast-action physical game in progress – batball, most likely.

51

Ping-pong, Su-Mueng thought. That's what we get down here. They don't play ping-pong in the Upper Retort. By Almighty Time, the games they play there!

But even ping-pong, the way it was played in Retort City, was interesting enough, workers' game or no. They secured a table and Su-Mueng took up his bat. The table was concave, like a wide, shallow bowl, divided by a thin screen of aluminium. Li Kim drained his beer, grinned, took up the ball and served.

They sent the ball ricocheting back and forth a few times. Kim was good, as Su-Mueng had discovered on many past occasions. The curved surface, of course, made a quick eye and hand all the more necessary; but that was not all.

Su-Mueng almost missed a return, just caught it, and hammered the ball over the left-hand side of the screen.

On crossing the divide it vanished in midair.

Kim vanished, too. But an instant later the ball came rocketing back at Su-Mueng and Kim, also, sprang back into view at the centre of the table.

This development demonstrated the speciality of Retort City: the ability to manipulate time. The table was divided into time-zones each of whose present moment was marginally out of phase with the others. More than quick reflexes were required – one needed to be almost psychic to anticipate where the ball would be returned from, or when. The phases could be adjusted so as to give a longer or shorter time difference, or more esoterically, rotated so that, for instance, the ball would be returned to the left and mysteriously come back from the right. It was even possible for the ball to be returned *before* it had been delivered.

And it was easy for the workmen of the Lower Retort to be technically extravagant with such toys. Technology was, after all, their life.

Kim was in fine form, flashing in and out of existence faster than Su-Mueng could follow or anticipate him. He might have done better if his mind had been on the game, but as it was his moves were confused with other thoughts. Kim won the first match and stood grinning at him.

"Same again?"

Su-Mueng laid down his bat. "Some other time, maybe. I don't think it's an even contest the way I'm playing today."

"Time-chess then? Each row on a different time gradient?"

Su-Mueng shook his head. Time-chess required such concentration, such a phenomenal memory, that he wouldn't have stood a chance.

"Oh. You want to relax more, maybe? A show? Or some girls?"

"Thanks, Kim, but there's something I want to attend to at home. I think I'll be getting along."

"Sure. Don't let me stop you. Well, in that case I'll be getting along, too."

Kim waved him a cheery good-bye and went bounding toward the gaudy awning of a trampoline emporium. Su-Mueng left the leisure area and continued on his way home.

Kim could never understand, he thought, what was on his mind. And his intentions would have left him aghast. Probably no one but himself *could* understand, and that went for either side of the divided city. People never did understand what was outside their experience, and for everyone but himself the other retort up – or, in the reverse case, down – the shaft was little more than a theoretical concept. . . .

The elevator swept down, past endless tiers of factories and workshops, past amusement emporiums and domestic precincts. Finally Su-Mueng left the elevator and made his way through a maze of tiny streets until he came to a neat little house merging with a dozen others in a jumbled, interlocking design. He put his thumbprint to the key and went inside.

His grandfather sat a table drinking a glass of fizzy mineral water. He was not really so very much older than Su-Mueng (so demonstrating another aspect of Retort City's mastery over time); to be precise he was twenty-six years older.

Su-Mueng gave him a perfunctory greeting, drew a meal from the dispenser, sat down and began to eat the synthesised rice, curried chicken and bamboo shoots.

"Interesting job today?" his grandfather asked, eyeing him speculatively. Su-Mueng nodded abstractedly. "Not bad." It still surprised him, even ten years after, how much casual conversation in the Lower Retort centred on work. The social system really did function as it was meant to: everybody down here had an obsessive interest in production, in making things. He was interested, too – after all, it was interesting – but with him that was not all. He did not neglect the wider vision that was denied to these . . . servants. . . .

He shovelled down the food and sat back, brooding. His grandfather switched on the wall screen. A technician was explaining how to set up a time delay circuit – a circuit that really did delay time, running a tiny fraction of the travelling "now" through a recurrent phase. Su-Mueng, already familiar with the technique, looked on without interest. Later there would be crude dramas, comedy shows, and so forth.

His resentment welled up. "You should see the kind of thing they screen in the *Upper* Retort," he suddenly said, loudly.

With a faint groan his grandfather turned to him, smiling derisively. "You're not going to start *that* again, are you?"

"But, Grandfather, wouldn't you *like* to see what it's like up there?" Su-Mueng asked. "Believe me, it's so *different*. They live so much better than we do . . . everything's so *luxurious*. You ought to see it."

The older man laughed gently, tolerantly. "Your father certainly has something to answer for," he chuckled. "You tell me they live better – I don't think so." He made a wry face. "No work, nothing really productive. Life would seem useless. I like it better here."

Yes, Su-Mueng reflected, that was precisely the secret of how the system was able to perpetuate itself: neither side of the split city envied the other. The inhabitants of the Leisure Retort were scarcely aware of the workers who served them, and the workers, in their turn, regarded the participants in the aesthetic leisure culture as idle drones who would probably have been happier doing something useful.

One might have expected that over the passage of centuries *some* sort of resentment would have built up. But Retort City had neatly circumvented this possibility, by the practice known as the Alternation of Generations – a weirdly democratic principle that for cunning and ingenuity was probably unique. For while the work and leisure classes were strictly segregated, their separation was on a non-hereditary basis. Each babe was taken from its mother a few hours after birth and transported to the opposite retort, usually to be reared by its paternal grandmother – who previously had surrendered her own child . . . now the babe's father or mother.

The arrangement was made even more perfect by virtue of the fact that the double exchange could be made simultaneously, even though in real terms a time lag of decades was obviously involved. This was because of the flexible phasing of the two retorts in time. *On the same day* that a couple parted with their new-born child, they received that child's own offspring . . . their grandchild.

It all had a simple, basic ethic: a man might be fated to spend his entire life in the Production Retort, but he had the satisfaction of knowing that his children enjoyed the luxury and sophistication of the Leisure Retort. Conversely, an inhabitant of the Leisure Retort who was obliged to send his children to a life of work and discipline in the Lower Retort was compensated by being able to educate his grandchildren in their stead.

In practice, however, such a rationalisation was unnecessary. Family attachments were weak; people harboured no feelings for the children they never saw, and experienced neither envy nor pity in regard to their lot. In centuries there had been no questioning of the social order, and very few defections.

"Come, now," Su-Mueng's grandfather chided, noticing his continuing long face. "Life's all right here, isn't it? Don't worry your head about life *up there*. Let *them* live it. This is good enough for me."

Su-Mueng didn't answer. Yes, he thought, it all ran perfectly – as long as the two cultures never met.

Which was why it didn't run perfectly with him.

For he was a product of one of those few defections, the only one, to his knowledge, in recent years.

His father was Hueh Shao, once an official of high rank – a cabinet minister, Su-Mueng believed – in the Leisure Retort. There must have been something badly maladjusted about Hueh Shao, for in a society where for centuries everyone had been faultlessly conditioned into accepting the long-established custom, he had been unable to bear the thought of sending his newborn son down into the Lower Retort. He had broken the law, secretly keeping the babe and representing it as his grandson sent up from below.

It seemed incredible that the deception could go undetected, let alone that Su-Mueng's absence from his proper place could go unnoticed, but somehow Hueh had managed it for ten full years. Then his crime had come to light. And the law was the law: there could be no exceptions. Su-Mueng, having been raised in what was probably the most refined culture the galaxy had to offer, and despite his tender years, had been sent down to live with total strangers in a different, cruder environment.

The first few years had been nightmarish; and though he had eventually adjusted to some degree, he had conceived a burning sense of resentment against the divided form of society.

And his father – the son of the man who sat opposite him –

had been punished. Was still being punished.

He glanced at his grandfather, realising that he was something of an embarrassment to the old man. He had arrived too late, like a messenger from another world.

They had no right to do that, he thought. They should have let me stay where I belong.

He got up from the table and slid aside one of the screens that divided their small dwelling, entering his minuscule home workshop. From a slender cradle he picked up a model of Retort City he had made: two bulbous glass vessels, cinched in the middle with a metal girdle, glittering within like a tinselled tree of metal components.

He had spent the best part of two years working on that model. It was not, in fact, a model – that was simply a disguise. It was a machine. He had put his utmost into it, all his skill, all his ingenuity and patience. One thing they did in the Production Retort was train you well.

This device was going to help him go back where he belonged, to his father.

He spent the next few hours checking it over with the instruments on his workbench. Eventually he heard his grandfather retire to his sleeping mat, followed by his gentle snoring. Su-Mueng made one last test, then slipped to his own cubicle where he changed into a loose, flowing tunic with a high collar. Then he put his model of Retort City in a cloth bag and left the house.

Minutes later he was on a high-speed elevator heading for the transporter end of the Production Retort, the great metal girdle through which all commodities passed to their destinations in the other half of the city. He swept past scenes that, in most circumstances, would have been fascinating: great shining structures of steel, aluminium and titanium that comprised an ascending industrial process terminating in the delivery area.

No one paid any attention to him when he left the elevator and picked his way across the shunting yards where big cylindrical carriers were pushed through the metal neck into the other retort. He went up a narrow passage, little used, that passed behind the main control junctions. He went through a series of doors and soon was in semi-darkness, climbing a spiral staircase that went up and up interminably.

A good deal of poring over maps and schematics, and a good deal of exploring, had gone into his discovery of this route. There were in fact several such routes: the area between the retorts was riddled with service access passages. All one needed was patience and the right equipment.

At length he came to the top of the staircase and into the galleries surrounding the massive coils that ringed the interior of the metal girdle between retorts. Already peculiar sensations assailed his body, warning him that he was approaching the influence of the stupendous field of variable time that separated the two societies. There was a feeling of tension across the bridge of his nose; his eyes went slightly out of focus; and his heart gave a cautionary jump.

If he had smuggled himself into one of the freight containers and got himself carried through that way, the steeply graded time difference would have killed him whatever precautions he took. This way, threading himself through the surrounding machinery like a needle through half a dozen holes, he stood a good chance. He took the fake model out of the bag and touched some studs fused onto its base. Within, a ragged pattern of subdued lights, amber, green and white, glowed.

He touched the studs again, making adjustments. The model had now taken control of his personal "now-moment", protecting him from the ravages of the energies in the giant coils; it would synchronise him more gently with the gradient, hopefully making the transition without injury to himself.

He went forward. He was in a place which, though cavernous, was so chock-full of machinery that it seemed like a solid mass. He squeezed between cabinets and stanchions, the hum of the machinery becoming louder in his ears. Once or twice he paused to make further adjustments to his device, and eventually the instrument told him what he already guessed.

He was through the time barrier -- synched with the time of the Leisure Retort.

There could be little to stop him now. He continued worming his way through the time-control apparatus, and finally was able to switch off his gadget altogether. But here he came to a slight difficulty. There were no maps or schematics of the Upper Retort available where he had been living for the past ten years. He had hoped that the receiving area would be, to some extent, a mirror image of the delivery area and that therefore there would be a descending staircase in a corresponding position to the one he had come up by. But where was it?

He searched, and located, not a staircase, but a small riding platform. This took him beyond the region defined by the metal girdle; he was in the Leisure Retort.

Below him stretched the retort's receiving area for all the goods supplied by the city's willing slaves. It was a shunting yard pretty much like the one he had left, except that everything appeared to be under cybernetic control and the canisters were already being broken open, their contents being transferred to smaller trolleys for dispatch to ten thousand different destinations.

Su-Mueng swung himself down from a gantry and strode confidently forward. He had nothing to fear. No one would stop him or question his presence; no one questioned anyone in the Leisure Retort.

And as he walked he already noticed, with a feeling of excitement, the difference between here and the place he had just left. The *air* was different; he had ceased to notice, during his long years as a worker, that everywhere in the Production Retort the air smelled faintly of oil and namelessly subtle industrial substances. Here there was only a faint suggestion of perfumes, of anything that pleased the senses.

Many times he had reconstructed in his mind the layout of the retort. He decided that he would not delay, but proceed immediately to execute his mission.

The next half hour was, to him, delirious. He passed through the gorgeous gardens and concourses that had grown faint in his memory. Past the people who went calmly, serenely, about their unhurried business – unfettered by any regime or timetable, but given to the abstracted, civilised pursuits of art and philosophy, of every kind of cultured subtlety. Here was life at the peak of refinement, a life incomprehensible to those in the Production Retort who had not been educated to appreciate it. But Su-Mueng *had* been so educated, and then it had been torn from him. As the aura of the Leisure Retort seeped into him his existence down below began to fade to the aspect of a dream. . . . Su-Mueng pulled himself together. He could not say how long he might manage to stay here, and he was bent on a task that to him was of great importance.

He entered a quiet part of the retort that was used chiefly as a precinct of government. No one accosted him as he walked through the fresh-scented corridors, decorated in shades of orange and lime green, that led to a group of apartments terrible to his memory: the place where his father was incarcerated.

Ten years ago he had witnessed the beginning of Hueh Shao's imprisonment. The Retributive Council had ordered that horror, in acknowledgement of the seriousness of his offence. Su-Mueng was not surprised to find the environs deserted; all would shun such a place.

The lock on the door was a simple one, though it could not be opened from the inside. Su-Mueng took a small device from his carrying sash, and after a little experimenting sprung it. Stepping inside, he found himself in a glass-walled foyer looking into the offender's prison: a dwelling-place something like that in which Su-Mueng and his grandfather had lived, but larger and much, much more luxurious. It appeared to be untenanted. Su-Mueng examined a panel set into the rear wall of the foyer, replete with strip-dials, access sockets and so forth. He took his time-phase controller out of the bag he carried, waved it in front of the panel and observed the interior of the glass vessels, touching one or two of the external studs.

Then he picked up a microphone and spoke into it, trying to keep his voice calm and unemotional.

"Honoured father," he said. "I know that you can see me, although I cannot see you. I am your son, Su-Mueng. I have returned to release you, if I can."

He put down the microphone and returned to the wall panel; on one end of the model city was a metal plate which he placed against the panel. Magnetic bubbles circulated in the plate, inducing control currents in the apparatus within the wall.

He would never be made to believe that his father deserved the punishment that had been inflicted on him. The Retributive Council had sentenced him to solitary confinement in past time. He was out-synched – his personal "now-moment" back-graded to minutes, possibly only to a few tens of seconds, behind the common "now-moment" of the Leisure Retort. His solitude could not have been more complete, and was scarcely mitigated by the concession that he was not permanently confined to his apartments – being permitted during certain periods to wander within a restricted area – for everyone's time was ahead of his; he could see them, but they could not see him, or hear him, or respond to him. He was like a ghost, moving among people who ignored him.

The mind of man, thought Su-Mueng, could not have devised a crueller exile.

The lights within the glass bottle flickered and raced. Suddenly the apartment shimmered and the artificially retarded time-field was abolished. There stood Hueh Shao, staring at him amazed, but like Su-Mueng forcing himself to adopt an attitude of dignified restraint.

The ex-minister bore a strong resemblance to his own father in the Production Retort – they were, in fact, of about the same age, a little under fifty – but the similarity was modified by the difference between the customs of the respective communities. He wore a long, wispy goatee beard and neatly cultivated mustachios that dropped down on either side of his mouth. The eyebrows were plucked, curved upward at their outer ends, and showed traces of cosmetic. The greying hair was carefully combed back, but was considerably longer than the cropped style affected down below.

He continued staring with steady eyes while Su-Mueng unlocked the inner door and stepped into the apartment.

"My son," he said, "what foolishness is this?"

And Su-Mueng stared back, unable to speak, unable to explain what foolishness it was. Incredibly, his thoughts had never ranged beyond this moment: the moment when he set the old man free. His father, a revered elder individual of intelligence and resourcefulness, would surely know what to do, his subliminal thoughts had told him.

Only now did he realise that those thoughts were the thoughts of a ten-year-old boy, arrested at the moment when the law had torn him away from that father. His childish adoration had never died. And only now, as he faced Hueh Shao, did it come home to him that his father was as helpless and resourceless as himself.

6.

A hush fell on the gathering in a quiet room in a derelict back street. Sobrie Oblomot stared at the tabletop, slightly embarrassed by the sympathy he felt emanating from the others.

"Sorry, Oblomot," the Chairman said, somewhat awkwardly. "But at least your brother died like a comrade. Went out with a bang. And took four Titans with him."

"That's not as self-sacrificing as it sounds," said Sobrie stiffly. "I'd commit suicide as well, rather than face what those bastards have waiting in Bupolbloc Two."

The Group Leader from Kansorn nodded. "The Titans have been coming down hard lately. I admit I wake up sweating sometimes. I never go without my s-grenade, either."

"I concur," said the man sitting next to him. He wore a mask and spoke through a voice modifier, being a person of such public prominence, and besides this of such importance to the League, that his anonymity was deemed essential.

"The League is reeling under the Titans' blows," he said. "Nearly three hundred people arrested in the past few months. The antipodean networks are practically destroyed. If this continues I fear for our whole cause."

The depression of the League members was palpable. The Chairman shuffled his feet and spoke more forcefully.

"There is less cause for alarm than many of you think," he told them. "The reprisals are a sign of our growing strength, not of our weakness. Remember what a low ebb we were at twenty years ago — at one time the Panhumanic League was down to about fifty members." He smiled ruefully. "Its very name was a joke. That was during the wars. But, after a long period of peace, we've been able to expand our activities and increase our influence. It was inevitable that there would be a Titan reaction to our successes."

"That's true," the Kansorn Group Leader said. "Our only problem is how we're going to meet it. Everything depends on our riding out the storm."

The Chairman nodded. "And that brings me to the main item of our remaining business. At the last meeting it was suggested that League membership should be barred to people of mixed blood. The reason for this, you will remember, was to protect our public image" – he spoke as if the words were distasteful to him – "so that we should not be characterised, as we have been, as an organisation of 'squalid freaks and sub-men'. I take it we have all considered the motion?"

"I'm against it," answered one voice with passion. "It runs counter to all our ideals. It suggests that we too consider other subspecies of mankind to be inferior. We shouldn't play the Titans' racist game."

"I'm for it," said the member from Kansorn, "merely on the grounds of tactics, as stated."

"How many of our people *do* have mixed blood?" Sobrie asked suddenly.

The Chairman answered. "The statistical department gives a figure of twenty per cent. A significant proportion – one which can give weight to anti-League propaganda."

"Propaganda is the least of our worries," grumbled the Kansorn Group Leader. "The Titan campaign against mixed blood is gathering pace, too. These half-breeds and octoroons give them a road leading right into the heart of the League. By moving against one, they move against the other."

"These people also see the League as their protection," Sobrie pointed out. "If we expel them, we can hardly count on their loyalty. We'll be twice as exposed as before."

"There's another aspect to the business," said the voice that had spoken previously. "Are we also to discontinue our contacts with the dev reservations?"

After a strained pause, the Chairman said: "We may, in any case, have to scale down our activities in the reservations. Titan supervision of these areas is so strict that they're becoming weak points in our networks – a number of agents have been apprehended trying to pass in or out. Even the imprisoned peoples have become wary of our approaches. Many of them have given up all hope of freedom and merely want to be left to live as best they can."

Several members snorted in disgust. The idea of any kind of future at the mercy of Titan hatreds, of Titan scientists and land-utilisation experts (always pressing to contract the already small areas "lost to True Man") was, to their minds, ridiculous.

They turned to the masked man, whose opinion, despite his anonymity, carried great weight. He pondered.

"The benefits to be gained from such a drastic step would probably not be great enough to justify the defying of our principles," he stated finally. "In the long run, it would do little to dispel the legend of the Dark Covenant."

Yes, thought Sobrie Oblomot, the Dark Covenant: the incredibly subtle, fantastically detailed scheme to destroy True Man that had supposedly been created hundreds of years ago by the combined evil geniuses of all the deviant subspecies then extant. The League was fairly sure that no such document, nor any document or plan even vaguely approximating it, had ever existed. But the beliefs that had grown up around it were elaborate and fascinating, and they were encouraged by the Titanium Legions. Popular belief had it that the Panhumanic League itself was but part of one of the Covenant's contingency plans, following the initial failure to exterminate True Man altogether and replace him by nature's mistakes . . . by the Earth Mother's mutants, sports and abortions.

It was the kind of inanity that made Sobrie Oblomot despair that the League could ever achieve its aim of bringing rationality to civilisation.

While the argument went on his thoughts returned – as they had returned every few moments since his hearing the news – to his brother Blare. Suicide, he thought bleakly. Gone in the glare of a fiery explosion when arrested by Titans. It would look fine in some annals after the battle was won, or on a monument in a better world. But here, in the squalor of an underground struggle, it seemed merely . . . bleak.

Blare had been an active member of the League for only a short time, and Sobrie was eaten up with guilt because it was he who had put his brother there. His hints, his persuasion, his appeals to reason, had won Blare over to the side of subversion. Not that it had been very difficult, but just the same Blare was too much of an ingenuous idealist, too much of a moral simpleton, to be successful in his work. Sobrie could see that clearly now. He shouldn't have pushed him into it. It shouldn't have been Blare who went up in that s-grenade. It should have been him, Sobrie.

The Chairman called an end to discussion and held a vote. The motion was narrowly defeated.

There was more discussion on tactics. It was decided to break up some groups and to scatter their members to various parts of the globe, where they were to remain inactive until further orders. The Chairman ended with a brief item.

"This is connected with your brother, Oblomot," he said. "As you may know, he was working with Rond Heshke, the famous archaeologist, on the alien ruins at Hathar. It seems that on the night your brother died, Heshke was taken by the Titans as well."

"I didn't know he was connected with the League." Sobrie frowned.

"He isn't. As far as we know Heshke is an upright citizen who holds a certificate of racial purity. We've learned that he was taken to Cymbel and put on board a private rocket transport. We're not sure, but we think the transport landed in the Sarn Desert."

"So?" Sobrie stared at him.

"The Titans have a secret research establishment there," the Chairman divulged. "They guard it so jealously that we haven't been able to find out what goes on in the place. But the fact that Rond Heshke may now be on the staff would confirm that it's connected with the alien interventionists in some way."

"And the aliens are also of interest to us," murmured Sobrie, nodding.

"Correct. We, as much as anyone else, would like to know who they were, where they came from, and what kind of beings they were. It's possible that racial fanaticism on Earth results from the antagonism between man and the alien. If so, our psychologists say that fear of the alien will have to be rooted out before hatred of other subspecies dies away."

Heads nodded. This theorem was known to them all. It did not, in fact, take a psychologist to be able to see it.

"I mention this only because we'd like more information, and it's proving hard to obtain directly," the Chairman ended airily. "Pass the word through your networks: does anyone know of any supplies being sent to the Sarn Desert? If so, what sort of supplies? By the way, the situation is made to look more interesting by the dramatic way Rond Heshke was suddenly picked up from Hathar."

64

The masked man gave a hollow laugh. "That means nothing. The Titans love drama."

"Yes, perhaps —" The Chairman turned suddenly as the door opened behind him, a pistol leaping into his hand.

But it was only the guard. "There's a report of Titan patrols in the area, Chairman. Thought you had better know."

"Thank you. You'd best get away, and tell the street observers to do the same."

The door closed behind the guard. "We'll wind it up now, for safety's sake," the Chairman ordered quickly. "Is anyone without a cover?"

Sobrie held up his hand. Being an artist, he was generally obliged to travel without being able to supply any particular reason. The others would all have equipped themselves with business or personal cover-motives for being in Cymbel. Most of them would be attending the World Economic Integration Conference Preliminary Hearings – the reason why Cymbel had been chosen for this meeting.

"Right, you leave first," the Chairman ordered. "If the guard's still here ask him to guide you past the patrols, and leave the city right away." He glanced around the table. "You'll all be notified of the next meeting."

Without ceremony Sobrie left the room. The others would follow at ten-minute intervals, the masked man leaving last of all.

The guard had already vanished. Sobrie checked the alley outside, then slipped from the derelict building. He strode quickly, almost running, until he reached the narrow defile that gave out on to a main thoroughfare.

The Titans had probably cottoned on to the fact that planet-wide conventions were a good opportunity for clandestine meetings, he thought. The Chairman would have to think of something else.

He saw one or two uniformed Titans about, but guessed that most of them were in civilian clothes. It was not hard to spot the tall, fair-haired young men by the cold, supercilious way they scanned the faces of passersby. Probably there were some people known to them that they were hoping to find.

He forced himself not to cringe as he walked by them. He was still worried by his obvious association with his own brother. But that had been weeks ago, and there had come no knock in the night. He could only presume that he had covered his tracks

65

well. And the one track he had not covered, Blare had covered for him. With an s-grenade.

He arrived at Cymbel's large transport field and bought a seat on the next rocket to Sannan. He had over an hour to wait, so he had a drink to calm his nerves, then decided the reception lounge wasn't the best place to be hanging around. He went into the district adjoining the field, wandered around for a few minutes and went into a public drinking lounge. After a couple more drinks he felt better.

There was really nothing to be afraid of, he told himself. The Chairman was simply being overcautious – a wholly admirable strategy. The Panhumanic League hadn't gone through over a century of experience without learning how to survive.

Several drinks later the rocket roared off from the transport field with Sobrie aboard. During the two-hour flight, arcing up above the best part of the atmosphere, he tried to sleep; but his head ached and he thought constantly of his brother.

It was an autumn evening when the rocket planed down into his native city of Sannan. It was a beautiful city, untouched by the dev wars. Rows of apartment blocks marched across the skyline, shining with muted colours in the slanting sunlight. Challenging them for prominence were the domes and towers of cathedrals, once centres of the old religions for which Sannan had been famous. These religions had been discouraged and were practically defunct now; the cathedrals were used for Titan pageants and for ceremonies revering the Earth Mother.

He left the transport field, his head clearing slightly in the fresh evening air, and took the tubeway to his own district. With a feeling of sanctuary he walked into his apartment, into the welcoming presence of Layella, the woman he lived with.

There were times when Sobrie felt weary of everything, weary of the cause he lived for, and felt tempted to give way to the persistent social pressure and to think: to hell with it, let's just live comfortably. What does it matter what happens to those others? That was how everyone else thought. The Titans, after all, are only working for the good of us, of real people. It can't be helped what happens to *those others*.

But then he would look again at Layella and renew his faith. She was one reason why he would probably never, not at any price, give up the cause. For Layella was of mixed blood.

Racially impure. Part Amhrak.

The percentage was not large – she herself did not know if it came from a grandparent or a great-grandparent, or even if some recessive genes had happened to come to the top – and because of her skilful use of cosmetics it passed unnoticed by the average citizen. Sobrie, by long loving acquaintance, was familiar with the differences and was eternally fascinated by the off-beat beauty they gave her. She had the small head and rounded cranium of the Amhraks – though not to an exaggerated degree – and the round, soft eyes, which she contrived to flatten a little with eye-paint. One dangerous feature was her ears, and therefore she kept them hidden beneath her hair, which was a soft, neatly cut shell of orange. Her skin shade was wrong, too – tending slightly towards Amhrak red – and for this she used a skin dye.

Other small differences in body proportion and stance she accentuated away by attention to her dress.

Provided life was quiet and uneventful she was safe. They could not marry, of course, since to be legally married both parties were required to obtain racial purity certificates, but otherwise no one of average percipience would know her apart from a True Woman.

But Sobrie knew – they both knew – that she could never pass muster if examined by the anthropometricians, the Titans' racial experts. They would come along with their tapes and calipers. They would measure her nose, her cranium, a hundred and one bodily measurements. They would apply a chemical to her skin to bleach away any dye and measure the skin-tone with a colourometer. They would take some hair to test for disguised crinkliness. They would strip her and observe the configuration of her bones when she walked, when she sat on a chair, and if they wanted to be exhaustive they would take a retinal photograph and run a chromosome test.

But more probably, he thought, they would do scarcely any of those things. They would not have to hunt so far to identify her. Some of these race experts, so he had heard, were real masters who by their own boast could "tell blood at a glance". They would take one look at her, and tell her to walk across the room, or else put a chair in the middle of the room and make her sit on it, noting the position of her buttocks. And they would know. And they would take her away and give her a painless injection, or perhaps worse, send her to the Amhrak reservation.

He flung himself down on a couch, exhausted by the content

of the day, and waited while she brought him a soothing bowl of soup. Then he told her about Blare.

Her sympathy, thankfully, was not embarrassing, as that of his League comrades had been. She knew his moods and his needs, as if by an instinct. She sat beside him, a hand touching his thigh, and said little.

He drank the soup quickly and leaned back with a doleful sigh.

"Layella," he said with difficulty, "we must part."

Her eyes widened with alarm. "Why?"

"It's getting too dangerous." He sought for words to make her understand. In some ways she was strangely oblivious to the danger that had surrounded her, almost since birth. Just like Blare, he thought with a sudden feeling of surprise.

He had steadfastly refused to let Layella join the League herself, though from their conversation she knew a good deal of his business with them – he was unable to refrain from sharing that side of him with his mate. But he had become more and more aware that he himself comprised the greatest threat to her existence. If he was pulled in, she would have no chance of escape.

"I don't want more people to go down on account of me," he said bluntly.

"*More* people? What do you mean?"

"Don't you see why Blare killed himself?" he said, looking up at her and trying to keep the note of agony out of his voice.

"You would all have to," she soothed. "It's necessary."

"No, no, you don't understand." He clenched his fists. "Blare is – was – not the suicidal type. He would have hung on for as long as he could. He's an optimist. He wouldn't have killed himself right away – and yet that's what he did. Almost as soon as they picked him up, before he could really have known how much they knew. He did it for *me*. So that he wouldn't be able to betray *me*. If it comes to that, I was the only person he could have betrayed. He had no direct connection with anybody else."

Both were silent for long moments. "You see why we must split up," he said heavily. "We've taken risks for far too long. I don't want to be the cause of your death, too."

"You're Blare's brother," she pointed out. "If they were suspicious they would have been here by now."

"How do we know they're not watching?" he rejoindered. "Still, we're a large family, and scattered. They may not suppose a connection. But that's not the point. They're still liable to get *me* some day. That's why you must go."

"No," she said with firmness, taking his arm. "You're my . . . husband, or whatever. I'm staying with you, to take whatever comes."

He stood up abruptly and paced the room, looking out of the wide window at the lights of the city, coming on in clusters and masses in the gathering dusk. "What a mess," he said, feeling his fatigue. "Those goddamned Titans – causing all this tyranny. There's nowhere you can go in the whole world and live like a free man."

"It's not really their fault," Layella said mildly, her expression open. "True Man, as they call it, probably didn't start all this. It was probably the Lorenes."

"No, it wasn't the Lorenes," said Sobrie agitatedly. "It was even before that. It was the aliens – their invasion started all this insanity. But for them, the races of mankind would probably be living in peace together. Before the aliens came, they probably *did* live in peace together."

She came over to him and stood behind him, her arms around his waist. At his back he could feel her voluptuous breasts, her head on his shoulder. From where he was standing he could see through the door into his small studio, littered with canvasses and plastic composites. Many of the paintings were of Layella. He thought bitterly of the studies of her he did not dare to paint, for fear that someone might see them: paintings of Layella without disguising cosmetic, in the nude, betraying the proportions between torso and hips. He thought of the children they did not dare to have, for fear of what might become of them.

Everything seemed hopeless. Nothing would be achieved in his lifetime; all the gains made by the Panhumanic League, important though they seemed within the League itself, were objectively trivial. Sobrie remembered what the Chairman had reiterated so many times: that they were working toward a goal that could not be achieved for several centuries; that their sights must be set that far ahead.

"Listen," Layella said. "I couldn't stand it if we parted. It would be too much of a blow for me. Leave the League if you like, if you can't stand it any more. We'll go away somewhere where we won't be traced to our life here. Not that I'm asking you to. But don't send me away."

"All right," said Sobrie. "Stay if you insist. If you can accept what it might mean. But I won't leave the League. The League comes before everything."

The meeting that took place far away, in a great castle some miles outside the city of Pradna, was far removed in style from the furtive sessions of the Panhumanic League.

The Titanium Legions were well-advanced in pomp; each high-backed chair bore a nameplate of titanium edged with gold, engraved with the name of its occupant. The table around which the chairs were set was of mahogany with inlaid platinum, while the walls were hung with tapestries depicting inspirational themes: representations of the Earth Mother with her strong, upright son; scenes of past glory – crucial moments in historic battles.

The Legionary Council of Generals convened once a year as a matter of course, or whenever Planetary Leader Limnich dictated. As he entered, all the Council members were at their places with eyes closed, deep in one of the spiritual exercises they all practised, especially during their sojourns at the castle. Planetary Leader Lemnich insisted on these practices among his generals; he knew them to be proven strengtheners of the will. They had been handed down from ancient times – but only to a privileged few – by True Men deeply experienced in spirituality.

"Attention."

Limnich spoke the word quietly but incisively as the big oak doors closed with a barely audible thump behind him. He was a man of below average height for a Titan, pale-faced, with a receding though blue-jowled chin, bulbous cheeks, and fish-cold eyes behind the large round lenses he preferred to more fashionable contact lenses.

The generals opened their eyes with a snap, summoned from their meditation, and stood to attention while Planetary Leader Limnich seated himself at the head of the table. Then, stiffly, they seated themselves again.

"Good evening, gentlemen," greeted Limnich in a distant, but conversational tone. "You must be wondering why I've convened the Council at this particular time, when our annual retreat together is so near. As you may guess, there's news of import. But first, I'll hear your reports."

One by one the generals gave a brief résumé. The accounts were

70

no more than recapitulations – each man commanded a vast area of activity and his real reports were massive documents handled by computers. But Limnich was never one to skimp on ritual. He bent his head to give closest attention to the remarks dealing with the pursuit of the Panhumanic League and the hunting down of racially impure persons, numbers of which still existed in normal society, even years after the last of the deviant wars.

"The work is long and arduous, but its conclusion is inescapable, gentlemen," he commented. "It must be prosecuted with unremitting vigour. Earth's destiny is dependent on a one hundred per cent purity of racial stock . . . but now to the main burden of my information tonight. . . ."

In the dimly lit chamber, whose illumination was supplied by shaded cressets, his voice fell to a dramatic murmur, the tone of voice he used on his extremely rare vidcasts – Planetary Leader Limnich was the most powerful man on Earth, but he was the power behind the throne, not the man on the throne itself. Ostensibly his title referred only to his command of the Titanium Legions. There was a World Racial President, a civilian, whom the Legions were sworn to protect. But in actuality Limnich handled nearly all practical affairs, and made nearly all important decisions, though frequently after conferring with the President.

"You all know of the work being undertaken at the Sarn Establishment, and of the discoveries that have been made there," he said, placing both hands on the table and directing his gaze at the shining mahogany. "You were all informed, by secret memo, of the mysterious disappearance of our first functional time travelling machine, together with Chief Physicist Leard Ascar and archaeologist Rond Heshke.

"The loss of Ascar is a blow to our efforts, since his genius was instrumental in developing time theory, but luckily developments had already reached a stage where we were no longer dependent on him. We were able to bring our Marks Two and Three machines into use fairly quickly, and a search was undertaken for the expedition that failed to return. It was established that the expedition had actually landed at its destination. But although the whole of the route covered in the flight plan was thoroughly searched, as well as its environs and possible alternative routes that might have been taken in an emergency, no sign of the machine itself could be found."

He paused, lifting his eyes to glower through his lenses like

71

some frightening goblin. "We formed the conclusion that the machine had been intercepted by alien interventionists, and its occupants kidnapped."

A tremor of consternation went around the table; backs stiffened. This was the stuff of which nightmares were made – the nightmares they had all experienced at some time since childhood, of strange beasts that dragged their victims into the abyss. And there was no abyss more bottomless, or more unknown, than that of time.

"Taking account of the possibility that the prisoners might be made to reveal the whereabouts of the Sarn Establishment, I immediately ordered the dispersal of its activities around the globe and the rapid building-up of our time travelling capabilities. With a determined allocation of resources, it was possible to bring to completion about twenty apparatuses and in the ensuing weeks a good start was made toward a more complete exploration of our time environment.

"Early on, one of the time machines was fired upon while in flight and destroyed. I had, however, given orders that the machines were only to travel in squadrons of three or more. The victim's companions gave chase to its attacker and pursued it *into the future*, where they lost track of it. Later, more signs of the aliens' presence were found, and revealed a situation of utmost danger. It seems that the aliens are extremely active in time, not only in the past, and in our present, but in the future also."

"The *future*, Leader? But how can that be?" One of the burly Titan generals, a man in his sixties, turned to Limnich in puzzlement. He was like many of these older Titans who had been born and bred in the deviant wars. His life had been one of conquest and heedless force, and he had difficulty in understanding these abstract concepts.

Limnich himself recognised his generals' limitations in the context of the modern world. Some of these old-time soldiers, he told himself, would have to be phased out. They would need to be replaced by younger men of greater sophistication. Men who understood theory, as well as the necessity for action.

"There is increasing evidence that the enemy has established a massive base some centuries in the future," he replied. "Presumably he believes himself to be out of the reach of retaliation there – *but he is wrong!*" His pale fish-like features suddenly burning with passion, Limnich thumped the table with his fist.

72

"Gentlemen, what I am trying to tell you is that we must once again put ourselves on a wartime footing. The second confrontation with the alien, which we have suspected would come one day, is imminent."

And the gleam of excitement that followed his words swept aside any incomprehension that might have bedevilled the Titanium Council. Here was one thing they did understand – and gloried in.

War!

"You will set to work in all your sectors to bring industry up to the pace of wartime production," Limnich told them more calmly. "Specific blueprints will be issued shortly, when we've trained sufficient technical teams in the new science of time manipulation. I've already taken the steps that will lead to the creation of time travel equipment on a large scale. This will result in new battalions being raised for the Titanium Legions: battalions trained and equipped to wage war across the centuries."

He paused again, and launched into the evocative language he could never resist on such occasions. "Mother Earth is once again calling her offspring to her defence. We must gird our loins, muster our strength, and strike before we're overwhelmed by the alien onslaught that we must assume is being prepared. There's no time for rest: we're entering upon a new era of conflict."

Limnich rose to his feet, paused with dignity while the assembly too, rose, and arms shot out, hooking themselves with clenched fists in the Titan salute. Then, without a further word, he turned and walked quietly from the chamber.

7.

Up until the second day the inevitability of death was something Heshke's mind had been unable to encompass. Stubbornly his thoughts had kept running in the same grooves as before, as though he were going to continue to live.

The second day was when their water ran out. The Titan tech officer, Lieutenant Gann, had suggested that they go searching for more, but Leard Ascar had ridiculed the idea.

"What for?" he sneered. "We'll probably find water – but one thing we won't find is *food*. We're on a dead planet." He stroked his pistol. "I'll tell you what I'm going to do. When I start to get too thirsty I'm using this."

And yet, though Ascar constantly licked his dry lips, his voice became cracked and he complained plaintively of thirst, he still had not killed himself. Heshke believed he knew why: the man's incredible brain was still at work, determined to wrest as much knowledge as possible from the enigma of time before he died.

They had dug a shallow grave to bury the dead Titan and now sat in the shade of the wrecked time traveller, talking desultorily. At first Lieutenant Gann had dwelt on the failure of their mission; but Ascar reassured him.

"It will only be a matter of weeks before they start sending out more probes. The truth will come to light. They're a thick-headed group, but it will penetrate in time . . . to start preparing for the holocaust."

Heshke shivered at the other's matter-of-fact acceptance of the calamity to come. "Then what chance have we of being rescued?" he enquired.

"None; don't harbour any hope on that score. They've got a whole planet and centuries of time over which to look for us. It's impossible."

"But they will find the alien civilisation?"

"Yes. Not as quickly as we did – it won't occur to them the way it did to me – but yes."

"But they might get shot down the way we were."

"Probably the first few will. Then they'll realise what it's all about, send out armed machines, and so on."

Lieutenant Gann came into the conversation, speaking in a hollow voice. "What we've discovered is almost too horrible to think about. This head-on collision you speak of – it's incredible! Are you *sure*, Ascar?"

"I don't understand it at all," Heshke admitted. "What are they, a time travelling civilisation? Have they found a way to make their whole society travel in time?"

Ascar shook his head. "It's even more than that. It's a whole biota – a world of biological life – that's unconnected with our own. I think it's a natural phenomenon, not an artificial one. Plainly, our own present – our own time-stream – is not unique. There are two of them – at least two – sweeping toward one another through four-dimensional space. When they meet it will be like God clapping his hands together, with all living creatures caught in the middle. . . ."

"You make it sound like the end of the universe!"

The physicist shrugged, then sighed. "Probably not. The end of time, maybe. I don't know; I just can't figure it out."

"Something else bothers me," Heshke continued after a pause. "The other civilisation is supposed to be only four centuries away from our own. But from the state of their remains, such as the Hathar Ruins, I would say they were *definitely* abandoned more than four centuries ago. It's hard to date these things, but an age of eight hundred, maybe even a thousand years, would strike me as more reasonable. It's an anomaly."

Despite his discomfort, a weird smile came over Ascar's features. "As a matter of fact that was one of the clues that turned my mind in the right direction. There are two ways that things can decay. They can decay with the progress of the Absolute Present – just normal entropy. But there's another kind of decay: the decay that sets in beyond the margin of the travelling time-wave – decay in non-time. Where the constructive forces of the present moment leave off, decay sets in. And at first entropy acts much more rapidly than in the present. So as you travel into the future things are falling to pieces very quickly. That's why living forms

75

vanish altogether, for instance."

They all pondered his words. "Of course," Ascar added casually, "as the now-wave draws closer things magically reconstruct themselves, as it were."

Heshke framed a further question, but before he could speak he was astonished to hear a whining sound from above. They all glanced up, and what they saw made them shout incoherently and cringe back in sudden fear, seeking the useless shelter of the time traveller.

Against the blue of the sky a metallic shape was falling rapidly toward them. They all fumbled for their weapons. Heshke was debating the futility of fleeing when the oncoming missile, with extraordinary agility, braked and came to a landing only a few hundred yards away.

"Looks like those damned aliens are back to get us," Ascar said through gritted teeth.

The Titan laid a cautionary hand on Heshke's arm. "They mustn't take us alive," he said evenly. "It's our duty to die by our own hands."

"Yes, of course," Heshke muttered.

But they all delayed the fatal moment. Heshke fingered his gun, secretly fearing to put a bullet through his own brain. Ascar snarled and stepped out a pace or two in front of the others, facing the vessel defiantly and hefting his weapon.

He's going to try to take one or two of them with us, Heshke thought, admiring the man's irrational courage. Perhaps I should do the same.

It surprised him that the machine standing out in the desert bore no resemblance to any of the time travellers he had seen. Vaguely, it reminded him of a space shuttle. It had an ovoidal shape and stood on its tail, supported by piston-powered legs. Just like something a human engineer would design that landed from space, he thought.

His perplexity was increased when a hatch opened and down stepped human figures. Ascar let his gun sag in his hand, while Lieutenant Gann started forward, his sharp features creasing into a frown of scrutiny.

"I'll be damned!" Ascar exploded.

Heshke started to laugh weakly. "And you said we wouldn't be rescued."

"Shut up!" snapped Ascar irritably.

And Heshke did stop. The men who came toward them were *not* wearing either Titan uniform or Titan insignia. Neither, for that matter, did they wear the familiar combat suits.

There were three of them (three of them, three of us, Heshke told himself with relief; they must be friendly) wearing what appeared to be light, one-piece garments without badges or symbols of any kind. On their heads were simple bowl-shaped helmets each sprouting a feathery antenna. And as they came closer they held up their hands palms outward, smiling and speaking in strange, singsong voices.

Heshke put up his gun; their friendly intent was obvious. Now he could discern their faces. . . . Their skin was sallow, virtually yellow; their cheekbones were unnaturally high, their noses somewhat flat, and they were slant-eyed. . . .

Heshke felt a long moment of uncontrollable nausea.

Beside him Lieutenant Gann drew in a loud, shuddering breath. "Devs!"

Ascar fell back to join them, his pistol wavering. "Who the hell are those animals? Where did they come from? What are they doing here?" He stared wildly, half out of his mind.

There could be no doubt about it. The newcomers were not of the race of True Man. True, their points of physical difference did not make them as grotesque as some of the races mankind had fought recently, but even so anyone with even a smattering of racial science could see that they were beyond the pale of true humanity as defined by Titan anthropometricians. In other words, they belonged to a deviant subspecies.

A loud report banged in Heshke's ears. Lieutenant Gann was firing, his face hard and determined. One of the devs spun around and fell, holding his arm where he had been hit.

Heshke drew his gun again, confused but thinking that he, too, should help fight the enemy. As it was he was given no time to fire. The two unhurt devs dropped to one knee and took careful aim with objects they held in their hands, too small for him to be able to see properly. He felt a momentary buzzing in his brain, before he lost consciousness.

Awareness returned suddenly and clearly, like a light being switched on. Nevertheless Heshke knew that there had been a lapse of time.

The strange surroundings took a few moments to become

familiar with. He lay, half reclined, on a sort of chair-couch, in a room that was long and narrow, decorated at either end with burnished gold filigree. He was alone except for a yellow-faced dev who stood by an instrument with a flat grey screen, and who gave Heshke a distant, rather cold smile.

"You—all—right—now?" he asked in a weird, impossible accent, pronouncing each word slowly and carefully.

Heshke nodded.

"Good. Solly—stun."

Heshke studied the offbeat face that belonged to his slim, youthful captor. These devs reminded him of something. . . . They were not representative of any modern subspecies, but he believed he had seen something like them in photographs of subspecies long exterminated. What had they been called? Shings? Chanks? It had been only a small grouping, in any case. It was perplexing to find them operating a time traveller – or spaceship? – now.

"Where are my two friends?" he demanded.

The other listened politely but did not seem to follow him. Apparently his grasp of the language was limited.

Nothing bound him to the chair-couch; he stood up and approached the dev threateningly. "What have you done with my friends?" he said, his voice rising to a shout.

The dev staved him off with a gesture; an elegant, flowing gesture.

"You–have–nothing–fear," he said, smiling broadly. He pointed to a table on which stood various articles: a pitcher, a cup, plates of food. Then he sauntered away from Heshke, opened a door Heshke had not noticed before, and left the room, closing the door behind him.

Heshke went to the table and sat down at the chair provided, inspecting the fare with great interest. From the pitcher – in passing he noticed its almost glowing glaze, its light, almost fragrant yellow colour, its fine shape – he poured a lemon-coloured liquid into the wide-brimmed cup and drank greedily. It was delicious; heavenly, unsurpassable lemonade. He drank again, and only then did he pause to examine the excellent craftsmanship involved in the cup. It was of a feather-light, bone-like material, but so thin and delicate that it was translucent. It had no decoration; its whole form was so perfect that it needed none.

He realised that he had fallen into the hands of a people who knew how to gratify the senses.

Next, being ravenously hungry, he attacked the food. It was a mixture of spiced meat, vegetables, and a near-tasteless mass of white grains he couldn't identify. At first he was disappointed to find the meal only lukewarm – he liked his food hot – but the flavours were pleasing and he gulped it swiftly down.

Afterward, his stomach satisfied, he felt much better. He could not altogether quell his alarm at having fallen into the hands of devs – but after all, this was such a totally mysterious situation.

And he was alive – and, hopefully, would remain so. Things were much better than they had been a short while ago.

He sat brooding, exploring the room with his eyes. Its shape was pleasing, he realised. A ratio of – four to one? Hardly the proportions he would have chosen, but somehow it worked; it was aesthetic. These people, dev or not, were artists.

He remembered Blare Oblomot, and felt a sudden pang for that rebel's protestations regarding the deviants. Poor Blare.

He became aware of a murmur of energy, barely audible through the floor. The room suddenly seemed to shift, to tilt. Then it became steady again.

Of course. He was in some kind of vehicle.

He paced the room, which was lined with horizontal slats of a honey-brown material, and stopped before the instrument the dev had been standing beside when he awoke. It was mounted on a pedestal, like a washbasin. As he came near, its flat grey screen glowed with neutral light; words appeared.

YOU ARE EN ROUTE TO INTERSTELLAR SPACE. The characters were neat, but functionally inelegant. There followed a diagram consisting of dots, some heavily, some lightly scored, superimposed by a series of concentric circles. An arrow left the centre and stabbed slowly out, jerking several times toward empty space.

Heshke guessed it to be a star map, but he was no astronomer and it meant nothing to him.

For a minute or two he waited, but the screen offered no further information. Just the same, he felt overawed. The civilisation to which he belonged could not undertake intestellar travel, though all the planets as far out as Saturn had been fairly well explored. It came as a blow to his sense of racial superiority to find these devs so advanced. Automatically his mind began seeking some explanation, one which would permit the fatal flaws of intellectual

79

or spiritual inferiority with which all dev races were supposed to be cursed.

Deep in thought he roamed the room. Absentmindedly he tried the door the dev had left by, pushing it and then pulling on a ledge set into the panel. To his surprise it slid open easily, vanishing into the wall.

He peered into an empty corridor, slatted with honey-coloured ribs as was his room, and hesitated. Had the dev mistakenly forgotten to lock him in? After a few moments he slipped out and proceeded along the corridor, feeling absurdly guilty and exposed, glancing all around him and expecting to be recaptured any second.

The corridor came to an end in a circular junction from which radiated other corridors. He hovered near the wall, peeping down each one in turn. Then he stiffened; a dev was striding out from a corridor to his right, unseen until this moment.

Heshke decided instantly not to put up any resistance and turned to face the dev, his arms hanging limply by his sides. The dev's stride broke for a moment and he looked at Heshke, his face speculative, interested. Then he raised his hand in what appeared to be some kind of greeting, nodded curtly and strode on past him.

Heshke looked after his retreating back, astonished.

"Citizen Heshke!"

Startled, he turned. The voice was Lieutenant Gann's. He came toward him down yet another corridor, at a near-run.

"Thank Earth I've found you," the Titan said breathlessly. "I was afraid they'd done something with you."

"You're free too?"

The other nodded. "So's Ascar. These fiends don't seem to care; we have the run of the ship."

"But why?"

"Who can say? A dev mind is bound to be devious, devilishly twisted. Probably they want to study us, catch us off our guard." He glanced around them, at walls, floor and ceiling, evidently seeking out spying devices.

"Where's Ascar?" Heshke asked.

"In his room. He's gone into a sulk, just sits there and won't co-operate."

Heshke looked carefully into the Titan officer's sharp face. He saw signs of nervous strain. Gann was intelligent, well-trained, but he was under pressure: in the very maw of hell, by his own doctrine.

"Let's keep moving," Gann said in a mutter, nudging his arm. "Probably they can't pick us up very well while we're on the move."

He guided Heshke down another of the corridors, pacing swiftly and talking in a low, furtive mutter.

"Keep your voice down," he warned. "Don't give them any more help than you have to."

"What have you found out?" Heshke asked.

"We're heading into interstellar space. Presumably this ship is equipped both with time-drive and some kind of interstellar-drive – but we always knew the aliens must have something like that. This disproves Ascar's theory, anyway: his theory that the alien interventionists are indigenous to Earth."

"Aliens?" Heshke queried. "But . . ."

Gann shot him a glance. "Isn't it obvious? *These devs are working with the aliens.* It would be just like them, too. They must be taking us back to one of the alien home bases."

Yes, thought Heshke, to Gann it would make perfect sense. It would enable him to resurrect his belief in the Earth Mother; to clear her from the charge of infidelity, of having given birth to two legitimate sons.

Doctrine apart, it made a certain kind of sense to Heshke, too.

"How can we be sure?" he said doubtfully. "Couldn't the devs themselves be responsible for all this?"

Gann didn't answer for a moment but glanced around him, gesturing with his hand. "I don't think so, Citizen. You've seen this ship, what a high cultural standard it has. I don't believe devs could have produced it. Besides, they would have had to invent the time-drive all by themselves, and that requires genius. Degenerate races don't have that kind of intellectual genius. Cunning, yes – but not genius. No, Citizen, the aliens are behind this."

Again, the Titan tech's reasoning sounded plausible. Heshke hurried to keep up with his swift strides. But, he thought, if Gann was right then that suggested that there was a conspiracy of cosmic proportions directed against True Man. . . .

Gann nudged him again, directing him down a side turning. They passed through a sort of foyer, or salon, where a number of devs stood before a large wall screen on which enigmatic schematics processed. They discussed quietly among themselves, and paused only momentarily to glance up as Gann and Heshke passed them by.

Gann remained silent until they were once more walking down an empty corridor. "Don't you know who these people are?" he said, his voice rising slightly. "No, perhaps you wouldn't . . . but I had plenty of instruction in race identification in training college."

"No," Heshke said, "I don't know who they are."

"They're Chinks," Gann told him. "The last group of them was supposed to have been exterminated five hundred years ago. Quite an interesting strain, as devs go. Tradition has it that their cunning was almost superhuman."

"*Super*human?" repeated Heshke wonderingly. "And yet you deny them intellectual ability?"

"It's more of an animal cleverness raised to a high degree. In devs the intellectual faculty is always perverted in some way, producing bizarre sciences and practices, yet it can involve extreme subtlety – in fact there used to be a saying: 'the fiendishly clever Chink.' "

Heshke found the phrase amusing and smiled, at which Gann shot him a sharp glance.

"It's no laughing matter. And you wouldn't think so if you fell foul of a Chink puzzle."

"A Chink puzzle? What's that?"

"One of their weapons, capable of incapacitating the nervous system. Just some kind of ingenious contraption made of wire or bits of metal, apparently. But whoever it's given to is instantly confronted with insuperable problems and riddles of such a nature that the mind is totally paralysed. The worst of it is that he can't be released until the puzzle is solved, which only a Chink can do."

With a deep sigh, Heshke decided that perhaps his amusement had been too facetious, after all.

"As you can see," Gann concluded, "these people are natural candidates for alliance with the aliens. Perhaps they were allied with them all along."

"Well, what are we going to do now?"

"Our duty is somehow to seize this ship if we can and take it back to Earth – and to the Absolute Present."

"But how?" said Heshke, overawed at such audacity.

"I don't know yet. I haven't finished reconnoitring. But there doesn't seem to be a very large crew."

"But even if we did take control – which doesn't seem possible to me – how would we fly it?"

"I can pilot a time traveller, and the alien version is basically the same as our own. We can manage it with Ascar's help, even if I have to kick co-operation out of him."

The Titan stopped abruptly. They were in a broad passage – a sort of gallery – one side of which was covered with silk screens adorned with delicate, trace-like figures of men, women and willow trees. The brushstrokes were sparse, economical but expansively eloquent.

"Well, that's the picture," Gann said. "We may as well get back to our rooms now. I haven't eaten yet and I'm hungry."

"Didn't they give you any food?" Heshke asked him in surprise.

"They left food of some kind. But I discovered the door was unlocked and decided action was more important. I've been all over the ship."

So that was why the Titan was so much ahead of him, Heshke thought. The man's devotion to duty was total.

"I don't think I can find my way," he said.

"I'll show you. Or else you can come back with me. It's probably not safe to talk in our rooms, though."

Heshke allowed the Titan to guide him through the corridors and to explain the general layout of the ship, which Gann had grasped in remarkably short order. Just before they parted, Heshke turned to face him, raising his finger as though bringing up a point of debate.

"You speak of Chink puzzles. I'm still wondering why they're content to let us wander around like this to plot and scheme. How do we know we're not on the *inside* of one of those puzzles, being manipulated?"

And the bleak, stubborn look on the face of the Titan showed that he, too, had entertained this thought.

It was hard to tell time on the Chink ship. The meals did not arrive regularly; they arrived as ordered. One had only to press one of the studs on the grey-screened pedestal and in a very short time a cheerful, smiling Chink would arrive, bearing a tray piled with the strangely spiced food.

Lieutenant Gann ate but sparsely and devoted all his time to finding a way to seize the ship, a project in which Heshke, none too willingly, was embroiled. They soon abandoned, however, the ban on discussions in their rooms. Heshke had grown tired of charging through corridors with the indefatigable Titan – and besides, he pointed out, the Chinks on the ship appeared to understand very little Earth Language. Probably the rooms weren't bugged at all.

Experimentally they tried stating some outrageously violent intentions, but their captors failed to come charging in as Gann had expected.

Both Gann and Heshke made efforts to talk to Leard Ascar. But the physicist seemed to have retreated even further into himself and barely acknowledged them. He ate vast quantities of the Chink food, calling for one dish after another, and seemed to relish Gann's disgust for his exotic tastes.

"Your ideas are all screwy," he growled when Heshke tried to talk some reason into him. "And so are your theories."

Heshke was taken aback. One could not help but have respect for Ascar's penetrating intellect, whatever the state of his mental health might be.

"I'm surprised to see you take this attitude," he admonished. "I thought you were as anxious to see the aliens defeated as anyone."

Ascar merely shrugged, scowling derisively, and continued engorging steamed rice in rapid spoonfuls.

They returned to Gann's room. "Plainly we can't count on him to help at first," the officer conceded reluctantly. "Nevertheless I don't think he'll refuse us technical assistance when the time comes. We'll just have to tackle the dangerous part by ourselves."

Heshke, whose enthusiasm for the venture was less than he cared to admit, sighed. "I don't see how we're going to manage anything. Just us against the whole ship!"

"It's our duty to try, whatever the odds. Besides, if we fail it will still remain our duty to kill ourselves before this ship reaches its destination. *We can't allow them to interrogate us.* So we have nothing to lose." Gann looked grim. "We'll have to kill Ascar, too."

"Very well. So what now?"

"I've evolved a plan." Gann reached into his tunic and drew out a sharp-bladed knife.

"Where did you get that?" Heshke asked, astonished.

"From the ship's kitchen. I wandered in there, and managed to pick it up before they shooed me away."

"It's still not much," said Heshke doubtfully.

"It's not all. Wait."

He unbuttoned his tunic and pulled up his shirt, then probed a spot on his abdomen, just under his ribs, with his fingers. "Feel there."

Heshke obeyed. He felt a hard lump under the skin.

"Something the Chinks don't know about," Gann said, with a note of satisfaction. "A vial of nerve gas." Suddenly he thrust the knife at Heshke. "Here."

"What?" Heshke blinked.

"Cut it out!"

Though squeamish with distaste, Heshke complied. Gann lay down on the chair-couch and took the cuff of his sleeve between his teeth. Heshke plied the knife, uncomfortably aware of the other's pain.

Fortunately the capsule was only just below the skin. It had been cleverly grafted in, so that the skin showed no trace of surgery. Heshke wondered whether all Titans were similarly equipped. Probably they were, he thought. It was like all the other thoughtful touches of Titan elitism: the blood-group tattooed on the inside of each man's arm, for instance.

The capsule came out easily, an egg-shaped spheroid slippery with blood. "Thanks," Gann gasped. "I could have done it myself, but I was afraid I'd make a mess of it."

"You're bleeding quite a bit," Heshke commented.

Gann looked around, snatched up a cloth that covered a small table and tore a strip off it with strong hands. He passed it around his waist, binding up the wound.

"That'll do for now. This is our plan of operations, Heshke." Gingerly he took the capsule, wiping off the blood. "Our first requirements are, one: weapons, and two: command of the control room. Now, most of these Chinks don't seem to carry weapons, but you've seen those ones dressed differently from the others – wearing blue jackets with high collars?"

Heshke nodded.

"I've reason to think that they do. They're probably officials or troops of some sort. There's always one of them standing guard outside the control room. You'll walk up to him and engage his attention. Then I'll come up behind – right?" He brought up the knife, going through the motions of grasping a man from behind and cutting his throat.

His stomach turning over, Heshke nodded.

"Right. Then we'll take his gun, and chuck the gas capsule into the control room. It's very quick-acting, but disperses after about half a minute, so we'll be able to take over. If anyone does come charging out before the gas gets him, we can simply shoot him."

"And what do we do then?"

Gann frowned. "Then, I'm afraid, we'll have to improvise. There'll still be the rest of the crew to deal with. But we'll be in a good position – at the nerve centre of the ship, and with plenty of weapons at our disposal. At least they'll know they've been in a fight."

Murder isn't my business, thought Heshke as they made their way toward the execution of Gann's plan. I'm an archaeologist, a middle-aged archaeologist. I wish there was some way out of this.

But there wasn't.

In a way their being devs made it easier; not like killing True Men.

But even killing a dog was unpleasant.

The thoughts were still spinning around in his mind when they came to the last intersection before the control room. Gann touched his elbow encouragingly and slipped off down a side passage.

Heshke continued on until he arrived at the demilune where some swing doors gave entrance to the control room. There was always a Chink standing here, like a commissionaire before the door of an expensive hotel. At the sight of him Heshke froze, momentarily paralysed. The Chink was so young, so affable-looking.

The young Chink turned and saw him, apparently noticing the stricken look on his face. Lieutenant Gann hove into view on the other side, a tall, comparatively sinister figure. He surreptitiously motioned to Heshke to get on with it; Heshke took a step forward.

And then, impatient with Heshke's hesitancy, Gann sprang. He hooked an arm around the Chink's neck, forcing his head back to expose his throat to the knife. Heshke's eyes bulged; he couldn't look, he couldn't turn away.

But just as the worst was about to happen something, a sliver of light, darted from the ceiling and struck Gann in the back.

Scarcely any change of expression came over the Titan's face; his body went limp, collapsing to the floor and nearly dragging the Chink with it.

The Chink recovered his balance and stared down at the body, his eyes wide with consternation. Then he flung open the swing doors and shouted something in a high-pitched, singsong voice. More Chinks came running from the control room, looking first at Gann and then at Heshke and chattering to him, their faces expressing commiseration, concern, regret.

One of them took Heshke by the arm and led him into the control room. He gazed blankly around at it, at the curved control panels sweeping by on either side, at the flickering screens whose rapidly changing images meant nothing to him.

His guide stepped up to one of the panels and began punching something out on a keyboard. After a pause words appeared on a screen over the Chink's head.

Ship programmed protect itself. Very sad friend die. Should have warned. So sorry.

Heshke nodded dismally, turned and walked back into the demilune, where a small crowd was still collected. For some reason Ascar arrived. He stood looking down at the dead Lieutenant, his expression unreadable. Then he suddenly gave the Titan hooked-arm salute.

"Salute to a brave officer," he said wryly.

"He *was* a brave officer," Heshke answered.

"Yes, I know."

Heshke felt unutterably weary.

He returned to his room and remained there for the rest of the voyage. He felt defeated, but oddly the death of Gann did not affect him as much as he might have imagined.

And neither did he kill himself. He had come to the conclusion that Ascar was right: Gann had been too presumptuous concerning the people who had rescued them from non-time. There was nothing substantial to indicate that they were hostile at all.

He slept, ate and slept, ate and slept until he felt rested. Eventually a Chink came and took him to the control room again. Ascar was already there; he gave Heshke a glance and a nod. He seemed to be familiar with the control room, as if he had made himself at home there.

The Chink pointed to a screen, and Heshke suddenly understood. He was being shown their destination. He stared entranced at the glittering shape, like an elongated hourglass, that hung suspended against ebon space, backed by hard, shining stars. A touch of the old apprehension came over him. Was this some alien stronghold, or—

Or what was it?

8.

Watching through the transparent wall of his spatio-temporal observatory, Shiu Kung-Chien saw the ship return from Earth and dock in the nearby sphincter. He could pretend no enthusiasm for the event; the ship's drive interfered with his apparatus and until the docking was completed he was obliged to suspend his current experiment.

He spent the time sitting patiently, drinking green tea and contemplating the dark, star-clouded universe all around him. He derived a satisfying feeling of insignificance from regarding it thus; a feeling that, as an organic, thinking being, he was a stranger in it. For it was an infinite expanse of non-time, a universe that had been made, in the first instance, without any time at all. Here and there localised processes of time had started themselves up, mostly weak, some quite powerful, proceeding in all directions, at all angles to one another. Occasionally they even met. They were accidental, small-order phenomena of limited period, but because of them life was able to exist.

On Earth, the most unhappy circumstance that could happen in the whole of existence had arisen: two distinct time-streams associated with the same planet. What was more, they were on a direct, head-on collision course.

Not that events of this nature were impossibly rare, especially in galaxies where the forces of *yin* and *yang* were so much out of balance as to cause numerous time-systems to arise. It was one good reason, in fact, for living in interstellar space, away from the traffic, as it were. Even so, Retort City itself had suffered a near-miss some centuries ago – a glancing blow by some entity travelling obliquely to its own time-direction. Shiu Kung-Chien still maintained contact with this entity: actually it was the object of his current experiments.

Pouring his third cup of fragrant tea, he noted that the space-time-ship had now slipped through the sphincter. No doubt the Earth passengers it carried would be full of hysterical pleas for assistance and he foresaw a tiresome time ahead. Personally he had opposed offering Earth any help at all, on the grounds that it might involve the full capacity of the Production Retort and cause inconvenience, particularly with regard to delays in the delivery of equipment he had ordered for his own work. But the other members of the cabinet, out of some sort of filial respect for the planet where mankind had been bred, had disagreed with him.

The meter by his side informed him that the incoming ship had shut down its engines. He rose, beckoning his cybernetic servitors.

"The area is clear. Let us begin."

The machines rolled across the work area to make final preparations. But Shiu Kung-Chien was interrupted yet again by a gentle introductory tone from the observatory's entrance door. Into the observatory came the sedate figure of Prime Minister Hwen Wu.

"Welcome to my retreat, honoured colleague," said Shiu Kung-Chien in a voice that bore just a trace of exasperation. "Your visit is connected, presumably, with the arrival of the ship from Earth."

The other nodded. "One of the passengers, it seems, is a scientist of some repute – no less than the brain behind the Terrans' recent discovery of time travel. He is hungry for knowledge. He'll certainly demand to speak at length with you."

Shiu Kung-Chien tugged at his beard and cursed. "So now I must waste my time conversing with barbarian dolts! Can you not give him someone else to vent his ignorance on? There are plenty of people adequate for that."

Hwen Wu affected surprise. "Let us not be discourteous, Kung-Chien. I am told that, judging by the character of the man, he'll insist on meeting our foremost expert in the field, and that is yourself."

"Oh, very well. But can't it wait? I'm in the middle of something important. I'm about to re-establish contact with the Oblique Entity."

"Indeed?" Hwen Wu clasped his hands within his voluminous sleeves. "I thought it had passed out of range?"

"So it had, using former methods. But this new apparatus of mine uses the principle of direct, all-senses contact."

"Is that not a trifle dangerous?" Hwen Wu inquired delicately. Shiu Kung-Chien shrugged.

"There's no particular hurry concerning the Earthman," the Prime Minister admitted after a pause. "He still has to be put through language indoctrination. Would the experiment be compromised if I were to stay and . . ."

"Watch by all means," Kung-Chien told him, "though there'll be little to see."

The servitors signalled that all was in readiness. Shiu Kung-Chien, Retort City's greatest researcher into the phenomenon of time, entered a glassy sphere which, though transparent from the outside, encased its occupant in apparent darkness. He murmured something, his words being conveyed to the cybernetic controller.

Hwen Wu gazed placidly on the scene. He saw the scientist go rigid, as though suddenly paralysed. His eyes stared sightlessly, his ears were without sound, even his skin no longer felt the touch of his garments or the pressure of the floor under his feet. His body remained, but his senses – and therefore his mind – had been transferred hundreds of light-years away in a direction which no telescope could show: obliquely in time.

"What shall we do, Father?"

Ex-Minister Hueh Shao looked at Su-Mueng, realising with a pang what a handsome young man his son had become.

"Do?" he repeated in astonishment. "This is *your* enterprise. What did *you* intend?"

Su-Mueng answered lamely. "I had hoped for your guidance, Father. Perhaps we could escape from the city, go to Earth."

"Hmm. Possibly, but I doubt it – and you obviously know nothing of the conditions there. We'd be unlikely to survive."

No matter; that had been the lesser of Su-Mueng's hopes. Vaguely, he had envisaged he and his father making a fight of it together. Suddenly getting over his initial stupefaction, he rose to the occasion and spoke with new resolve.

"Then return with me to the Production Retort. It's honeycombed with little-used areas, deserted spaces. I'll find a hideout for you there."

"What, exchange one prison for another? Where's the advantage in that?" The older man frowned.

"No, that's not it." Abruptly the real issue that lay before him crystallised in Su-Mueng's mind; the heat of passion entered his

91

voice. "There's work to be done. We must work to overthrow the structure of society!"

His father stared at him as though he had gone mad. "Do you know what you're saying?" he exclaimed in a shocked whisper.

"But isn't that why you committed your crime and tried to save me from my fate?" Su-Mueng rejoindered. "Do you not feel the injustice of our way of life? One part of the population being forced to content itself with production, otherwise enjoying only crude entertainments, which the other part leeches off this work force?"

"But we're maintaining the highest state of civilisation!" spluttered Hueh Shao. "The arts and the sciences have been carried to the peak of sophistication here in the Leisure Retort, to say nothing of the graciousness of our life-style. How could we devote ourselves to this if we had to spend time producing material things for ourselves?"

Su-Mueng was taken aback by this response, which was not what he had expected. "The inhabitants of the Lower Retort could also enjoy what we have here, if they were given the opportunity," he said. "It's unfair that it should be denied them. *All* should share, in production as well as in higher things."

"But then neither production nor refinement could be carried as far," his father replied with a wave of his hand. His voice fell, became sombre. "I confess that my motives in keeping you in the Leisure Retort were purely selfish. I'd wanted my son to live as I'd lived. No feeling of a general injustice entered my mind – that, presumably, would only occur to someone who saw both sides of the divide."

"Then come down to the Lower Retort and see for yourself!"

Hueh Shao sighed. "It seems that I set in train more than I dreamed when I hid you in my secret apartments. Social revolution, now!"

"Are you agreed, then? If we leave quickly perhaps no one will learn of your escape for some time."

"They know of it already," Hueh Shao told him, indicating the panels by the door. On one of them an amber light glowed. "The time-displacement machine has reported your interference of it."

Su-Mueng whirled and gasped. Running to the panels, he pulled free the model of Retort City he used as a time-control and brandished it vigorously.

"Quickly – before they get here. Perhaps I can out-phase us with this – make us invisible!"

Hueh Shao's face was a mixture of sadness, pity and regret. He followed his son into the corridor outside the apartment, where Su-Mueng fiddled desperately with his time device, producing a chiaroscuro of flickering lights.

"There!" he pronounced with satisfaction. "We're back-phased a full half minute. If we move fast we can be in the Lower Retort within the hour."

Again Hueh Shao hesitated, and then seemed to come to a decision and nodded, moving with Su-Mueng through the scented passages, staying within the field of his gadget. Su-Mueng walked rapidly, excitedly, but even before they left the section they encountered what the older man had known they would encounter, but which he had optimistically supposed they would not.

It was a rare sight in the Leisure Retort: four citizens in the garb of law enforcement officials, looking oddly severe in the tight-fitting blue jackets and high collars, coming along the corridor with calm self-confidence.

Their leader carried a small cylinder which he held before him like a torch. Even as he noticed this Su-Mueng felt a wave of dizziness and realised with dismay that he'd been phased back into normative time. His hand darted to his double retort, but then went limp as he recognised the greater power of the other's instrument.

The leader looked from one fugitive to the other, a hint of recognition crossing his features. "Would you kindly accompany us?" he asked politely. "Regretfully, we must presume that you're in infringement of a city ethic."

The blue-jacketed men turned and retraced their steps, leaving their prisoners to follow them of their own accord. Su-Mueng was sick to think how futile all his work had been.

From the moment when they passed through the ship's outer doors and into the incredible space city, a phantasmagoria of rich impressions greeted Rond Heshke and Leard Ascar. The ship they had been travelling in, Heshke realised, was austere and functional compared with the voluptuous standards of these people.

The air was invigoratingly fresh and laden with captivating scents. They had emerged from some kind of dock into which the ship, apparently, fitted snugly; and the spectacle before them was bewildering in its complexity. Level gave way to level and split-level; screens and interrupted walls ran hither and thither with the complexity of a maze, offering glimpses of gardens and parks arrayed in riotous colours.

The place breathed the essence of luxury. Blooms and delicate orchids flowered everwhere, springing from walls and ceilings. It was like being in some primitive conception of Heaven.

A Chink led them through a low archway and gestured to them to be seated in a carriage that appeared, to Heshke's astonished eye, to be made of green jade. The carriage moved silently along meandering pathways, giving Heshke a chance to observe the people of the city. Their styles of dress were varied; most common among the men, however, was a long, flowing silk robe with enormous sleeves. The older men generally affected long, sparse beards, adding yet more strangeness to their slanted, scarcely human features.

The dress of the women was much more diverse. Some swathed themselves in voluminous silk, others wore short, revealing split skirts or scarcely anything at all, and all wore flowers in their invariably black hair. Despite his natural revulsion for devs, Heshke gazed fascinated at their alien beauty, and at the graceful, sedate fashion in which both they and the men carried themselves.

More and more his "educated" attitudes as regards deviant subspecies were coming crashing to the ground. It was impossible to claim now, as Lieutenant Gann had, that all this was the creation of extraterrestrials. Quite obviously these Chinks had a superb sense of beauty – something which, in Titan doctrine, only True Man possessed. He thought of Blare Oblomot, who would not have been at all surprised by it.

Ascar, he reflected, had been right yet again: their ideas had been all wrong. And Ascar was certainly no underground sympathiser. He turned to him to make a comment; but Ascar was taking no notice whatsoever of his surroundings. He sat looking blankly at his lap, his face wearing his customary sullen scowl.

It just doesn't get through to him, Heshke thought wonderingly. He's all intellect – he's blind to everything that isn't abstract.

The carriage entered a set of vertical guide rails that took it up, amid masses of perfumed foliage, to another level. Here there were no more gardens; the prospect was that of an endless summerhouse whose apartments were partitioned by flimsy, movable screens, exquisitely decorated. At their conductor's request they left the carriage and walked a short distance through this open-plan habitat. Heshke noted the sparsity of furniture; indeed, too much furniture would have entirely spoiled the light, airy effect. Everything here in this city, it seemed, was arranged to provide perfect harmony.

They rounded a corner and came to a stop in a fairly small room where a tall, bearded old man regarded them with cold detachment. On a table beside him were several bowls and an assortment of slender needles, some gold, some silver. Unrecognisable apparatus stood on the other side of the table, while on the wall behind was an apparently normal television screen.

The old man uttered some quiet words, and with much dignity motioned Heshke to recline on a nearby chair-couch.

Heshke did so with reluctance, and then felt a sudden panic as the Chink took up one of the long, slender needles. All his repugnance of devs came flooding back, and his mind filled with fears of hideous, infinitely cunning tortures. Seeing his terror, the old Chink paused, head inclined.

Ascar spoke, struggling with unfamiliar syllables. To Heshke's boundless admiration he had actually succeeded in picking up a few phrases of the impossibly difficult language. He listened to the Chink's reply, spoken slowly and clearly for his benefit.

"Relax," Ascar said then to Heshke. "He's not going to hurt you. It's some sort of processing. They're going to teach us the language."

Partially reassured, Heshke leaned back. The oldster approached, muttering something, and touched him just behind his ear. Where his fingers touched, Heshke seemed to go numb. Then the Chink applied the needle he was holding; from his action Heshke knew that he was inserting it under the skin, deeper and deeper.

Into his brain!

He fought not to feel frightened. The Chink, with the assurance and solicitude of a skilled doctor, used about a dozen needles on him in all, in various parts of his body: chiefly around his head, neck, hands and arms. But as the treatment progressed a curious soothing feeling overcame him and his fears vanished. Finally the oldster stepped away and returned a few moments later, slipping some earphones over his ears and some goggles over his eyes which plunged him into blackness. He heard the snap of a switch.

And Heshke fell instantly asleep.

He awoke, he did not know how much later, to find the old man deftly pulling the needles from his skin. Ascar, too, had just finished his treatment. He rose from a second chair-couch, smiling sardonically at Heshke.

"Excellent," said the old man. "And may you both be honoured guests in our city."

He had spoken in the singsong Chink tongue – and yet Heshke had understood it.

"This is really remarkable!" he exclaimed. But the other waved his hand.

"You're still speaking in your own language," he intoned. "Try to find the *other* tongue in your mind – and speak again."

Puzzled, Heshke tried to do as he was instructed, turning his attention inward as he spoke. "I was merely praising the effectiveness of your treatment," he said. "I'd like to know how you did it."

And then, while he was speaking, he found it: the "other tongue" – lying alongside his own in his mind, ready to seize his larynx and tongue and to express his thoughts, as automatically and faultlessly as he used his own language. His last few words came out in the language of the Chinks.

It was strange at first – like being able to switch to another vidcast channel at will.

The old man smiled politely. "The principle is quite simple," he explained. "A computer-programmed language course was fed into your mind at high speed while you were unconscious, so that for every word or phrase of your own language, the speech centre of your brain now contains the equivalent word or phrase of our language."

"That's pretty impressive," Ascar interjected, also speaking flawless Chink. "I've never heard of anything like that before. I wouldn't have thought it was possible – not in such a short space of time, anyway."

Heshke listened fascinated to the way the foreign syllables flowed off Ascar's tongue – and was just as fascinated at his ability to understand them.

"The brain's capacity to absorb information at computer speed is not, I believe, known to your people," the old man admitted. "We're able to achieve it with the assistance of an ancient technique called acupuncture." He indicated the needles that lay on the table. "By inserting these fine needles at particular points

96

under the skin we're able to deaden or stimulate the nerves selectively. By this means we open the requisite pathways to the brain so that it's able to assimilate data at a much faster rate than normally – and there are also many other uses for acupuncture."

"But that seems such a primitive way of going about things," Heshke commented, staring at the needles. "Your apparatus is hardly sophisticated."

"The technique depends more on knowledge and skill than upon technology," the old man replied. "It is a very old practice, but it's been vastly refined and extended by us here in Retort City. It's said to have been invented originally by the ancient philosopher Mao Tse-Tung, who also invented the generation of electricity." The Chink smiled tolerantly. "But these legends are not, of course, reliable; they also tell of him driving out the evil demons Liu Shao-Chi and Lin Piao."

Ascar grunted and cast a sarcastic glance at Heshke. "You're right – history tells nothing but fairy stories."

Heshke ignored the gibe. "I take it your people have a reason for bringing us here," he said to the old man. "When will we learn what it is?"

The other sighed. "Ah yes, very distressing. But that's not my province. You'll have to meet representatives of the Cabinet – perhaps even the Prime Minister himself. Have patience."

"Patience be damned," growled Ascar, finding Retort City curses not strong enough for his liking. "When am I going to meet your physicists?"

In view of the seriousness of the offence, Prime Minister Hwen Wu himself presided over the court. With him sat two lesser ministers, and at a table to one side were the court's advisers, experts in logic and law.

Hueh Shao was brought in first and offered green tea, which he refused. He pleaded guilty to attempting to break his confinement, and added that he had intended to go into hiding in the Production Retort, where he would be helped by his son. His voice betrayed an inner weariness, as he spoke quietly and calmly.

Hwen Wu found the proceedings disturbing to his inner peace. There seemed to be only one possible judgement that could be made in the case of the man who once had been his close friend.

"One further statement I wish to put before the court," Hueh

Shao continued, "and that is that my son Su-Mueng should be absolved from guilt. It was with my encouragement that he agreed to guide me to the Lower Retort, and in so doing he was prompted by filial duty – he looks upon me as other men look upon their grandfathers. Furthermore, his entire aberration springs from my own actions. But for my former crime he would have lived happily and blamelessly as a production worker, with no knowledge of any other life. In my opinion, any punishment inflicted upon him would be unjust."

A logician raised his hand, was recognised and rose to speak.

"The accused commits an inconsistent statement with his tale of how he induced his son to guide him down to the Production Retort," he said in a low, melodious voice. "The facts are these: Hueh Shao and Hueh Su-Mueng *were* apprehended while leaving the area where Hueh Shao was incarcerated. Hueh Shao admits to this. But as regards his statement of his intentions. Hueh Shao must certainly *have known* that he and his son would be apprehended before leaving the Leisure Retort – although Hueh Su-Mueng, possibly, did not. Hueh Shao couldn't have intended to do something which he knew to be impossible, and therefore his intentions were otherwise."

"And what were his intentions?" Hwen Wu queried.

"Taking everything into account, it would appear that Hueh Su-Mueng appeared unexpectedly in his father's apartment and released him from his time-displacement. Hueh Shao was then in a quandary; he knew his son's scheme to be impossible to execute, and that his son was laying himself open to severe punishment. From that moment on his foremost intention became to spare his son from this punishment – remember the unusual bond that exists between these two, unnatural though it might seem to us. He pretended to fall in with Hueh Su-Mueng's plan, in order that he might thereby represent himself as its part-instigator and remove some of the guilt from his son's shoulders."

Hwen Wu turned to the accused.

"Do you admit to this version of events?"

Hueh Shao nodded; the logician had mercilessly exposed his motives.

"Hueh Shao's following statement, however, stands up to examination," the logician continued. "Hueh Su-Mueng's aberrated state of mind *is* to be laid entirely at his door. But whether we should conclude from this that no punishment devolves upon

98

the younger man is an entirely different matter. One cannot dismiss the principle of personal responsibility so lightly."

The Prime Minister listened carefully to these pronouncements, considering them from all angles. Finally he turned to the accused again.

"I find you guilty of cooperating in your own escape, but not of instigating your escape," he said. "Your actual infringement, in this particular instance, of a city ethic is not an enormous one, but that's not the issue before us here. The issue is that your original crime, one of truly serious proportions, has surfaced again. You've created an individual of apparently irremediable criminal tendencies – already, in his preliminary statements, your son has expressed himself as being totally opposed to the social structure."

He fingered the tendrils of his beard, contemplating. "Your crime is unforgivable because it strikes at the roots of society," he proclaimed. "If allowed to gather force it could destroy the civilisation we enjoy here in Retort City. Nevertheless, your sentence was a lenient one, initially, because it was the first case of its type to occur for many centuries. We must now withdraw that leniency. I regret that I must sentence you to loss of life." He looked calmly at Hueh Shao. "Do you agree with the sentence?"

Hueh Shao nodded. He could almost see what was in the Prime Minister's mind. The sentence was not merely on himself; it gave Hwen Wu a way of punishing Su-Mueng without directly punishing him. The principles of fairness and justice were both satisfied, even though they were in conflict.

"Then let the sentence be carried out immediately."

Hueh Shao turned and walked out through a door to his right.

A minute or two later Su-Mueng took his place before the court. He listened to the formal charge, pleaded guilty, but in his following statement firmly absolved his father of all guilt in the matter.

Meantime, in a nearby room, Hueh Shao relaxed into a chair-couch and was handed a bowl of refreshing green tea.

The bowl was of the most delicate porcelain and its embossed design, a mere tracery when touched by the fingers, was of a style he particularly admired. He sipped the tea, enjoying its fragrance. A feeling of numbness, not particularly unpleasant, came over his limbs as the poison in the tea took effect. He laid the bowl down on a nearby low table, the tea still unfinished, and quietly died.

99

In a cold voice Hwen Wu accepted Su-Mueng's plea and explained the verdict and sentence that had just been passed on his father. "The sentence," he added, "will by now have been carried out."

Su-Mueng's reaction to this news inflicted the whole court with a faint feeling of revulsion, for it demonstrated the emotional bond that existed between two men who should never even have known one another. Su-Mueng went deathly white and sagged as though punched in the stomach. He recovered himself with difficulty, drawing himself erect, his face still grey, and looked Hwen Wu straight in the eye.

"Damn you," he said in a strangled voice. "Damn you all. Your whole system is evil – and one day it will be destroyed. . . ."

The President of the Court nodded. "We're acquainted with your opinions, and of their causes. We're aware also that your attitudes are intractable, which raises the problem of what we're to do with you. Punishment is inappropriate, because insofar as punishment is deserved it's already been inflicted in the form of your knowledge that your actions have led to your father's death. We cannot permit you to live in the Leisure Retort, since that would transgress the law; yet if we return you to the Production Retort, which is your proper place, you'll no doubt continue to cause trouble. So the question remains, what are we to do with you . . . ?"

9.

Leard Ascar had been obsessed, from an early age, with only one question.

The question of time.

He could remember the day – it had been his tenth birthday – when the full force of the enigma had first struck him. The dilemma, the paradox, the impossible, irreconcilable paradox. The transient present, moving from a past that vanishes into a future that appears from nowhere. And even more perplexingly, what he later came to know as the Regression Problem: how can time "pass" without having "time" to pass in?

These enigmas drove out all his other interests. He read everything he could understand on the subject, and then studied physics and mathematics so as to understand what was left. He was precocious, ahead of his class in all the subjects he took. He never made any friends, but could have had a brilliant career in almost any branch of physics, had he not preferred to devote himself to unsuccessful, self-financed researches into the nature of time. Among more conventional minds he gained a reputation as a crank, an oddball, and his experiments had regularly ground to a halt for lack of any further money.

Then he had come into contact with the scientific establishments of the Titanium Legions and they, to give them their due, had made it possible for him to continue his work. Following the victories over the deviant subspecies there had been a splurge of boastful expansionism in the sciences, a feeling that True Man could achieve anything. Not only Ascar but real cranks, near-psychotics with the most extraordinary and fanciful theories, had been allotted funds to bring their ideas to fruition. And so he had made some small progress, until that incredible day when the real nature of the captured alien vehicle had become evident.

That day had been a climax in Ascar's life. A second climax came on the day he was introduced to Shiu Kung-Chien, the foremost expert on time in a city that had mastered nearly all its secrets.

That he had been trained to regard individuals of Shiu Kung-Chien's race as subhuman did not bother him. He would gladly have sat at the feet of a chimpanzee if it could have taught him what he wanted to know.

He sat across from the master physicist, beside whom, on a lacquered table, was a pot of the steaming green tea the man never seemed to stop drinking. Around them was Shiu Kung-Chien's observatory which, so he understood, explored both space and time: on one side a curving, transparent wall giving a view of empty, sable space, on the other a neat array of apparatus whose functions Ascar could not divine.

Shiu Kung-Chien himself Ascar would not have picked out among his compatriots – but then these Chinks all looked alike to Ascar. His dress and appearance were modest: a simple, unadorned silk gown tied at the waist with a sash, the long, silky beard worn by many of his generation. But his fingernails, Ascar noted, were unusually long, and painted. It seemed that Shiu did almost no physical work himself; all the equipment he used, though designed by him, was constructed elsewhere, and thereafter was set up and attended by the robot mechanisms that now busied and hummed at the other end of the observatory.

"Yes, that's quite interesting," Shiu Kung-Chien said. He had been listening politely while Ascar tried to give him a rundown on his own ideas and what had led up to them. They'd been forced to resort to verbal descriptions – Ascar's own equations, as it turned out, were adjudged near-useless by Shiu, and those he offered instead were incomprehensible to Ascar. Seemingly the type of mathematics he used had no equivalent in Ascar's experience, and even the acupuncture assisted language course was of no help.

Ascar folded his arms and sighed fretfully, rocking back and forth slightly on his chair. "Up until recently my mind was clear on the subject. I thought I'd got to the bottom of the age-old mystery. But since I discovered *another* 'now' – another system of time moving in the opposite direction – I've been in confusion and don't know what to think. The picture I'd built up is really only credible if the Absolute Present is unique." He shot Shiu a hard glance. "*You* tell me: is the universe coming to an end?"

Shiu's seamed face showed amusement and he chuckled as if at some joke. "No, not at all. Not the universe. Just organic life on Earth. To be more precise, *time* is shortly due to stop on Earth."

He waved a hand and a cybernetic servitor rolled forward with a fresh pot of tea. "You know, you haven't quite disposed of the Regression Problem, although you appear to think you have."

Ascar frowned. "Let's make sure we're talking about the same thing. The Regression Problem points out the apparent impossibility of passing time. It's defined thus: take three consecutive events, A, B and C. One of these events is occurring 'now' and the other two are in the past or the future. Let's say that B is 'now', so that A is in the past and C is in the future. But there must have been a time when A was 'now' and B and C were in the future, and likewise there will be a time when C is 'now' and the other two are in the past. So we can draw up a table of three configurations of these three events, giving nine distinct terms in all. But we can't stop there: if we did there'd be three simultaneous 'nows', and there can only ever be one 'now'. So we must select one of these configurations and assign our own 'now' to it – this gives us a second-order 'now' related not to a single event but to a dynamic configuration of all three events: the one containing the real location of 'now'. But we can't stop there, either. Each one of the three configurations can in turn claim a second-order 'now', by virtue of the fact that the 'now' is moving. So we have to draw up a new table where the first table is repeated three times, the A-B-C groups number nine, and the single events themselves are permutated to twenty-seven, all this being encompassed by 'third-order time'. The process can be repeated to the fourth-order, fifth-order, and *ad infinitum* time."

Shiu waved his hands at Ascar, suddenly impatient with the exposition. "I'm fully conversant with all the arguments," he said. "But what made you think you'd resolved the paradox?"

"Well," said Ascar slowly, "when we actually travelled into the past and into the future and discovered there was no 'now' there, I simply assumed that the whole argument was fallacious. The facts showed that there *was* no regress."

"But did you not bother to ask yourself *why* the regress did not occur?" said Shiu acidly. "No; you merely rushed in like a schoolboy and forgot about the matter."

103

Ascar was silent for long moments.

"All right," he said, "where did I go wrong?"

"Your basic mistake was in presuming time to be a general feature of the universe," Shiu told him, bringing out his words carefully and emphatically. "You imagined the Absolute Present as a three-dimensional intersection of the whole of existence, traversing it everywhere simultaneously, much like a pickup head traversing a magnetic tape and bringing the images it contains to life. Agreed?"

"Yes," said Ascar, "that's a pretty good description."

"But don't you see that if you adopt that picture then *the Regression Problem remains?*"

"No," Ascar answered slowly, "because the time intersection passes each instant only once —"

He stopped suddenly.

"Yes, you're right," he resumed heavily. "I can see it now. There'd have to be an infinite number of identical universes, one for each instant in our own universe, varying only in that the Absolute Present — the time intersection — was in a different part of its sweep. Every instant, past, present or future, would at this moment have to be filled by an Absolute Present somewhere among those universes."

"And beyond that," Shiu continued for him, "would have to exist a further set of universes numbering infinity raised to the power infinity, to take care of the next stage in the regression. Already we're into *transfinity*."

Ascar nodded hurriedly. "All right, I accept that. I also accept that the facts have shown my model to be wrong. *So what's the truth?*"

"The truth," said Shiu, "is that the universe at large *has no time*. It's *not* 'now' everywhere simultaneously. The universe is basically, fundamentally static, dead, indifferent. It has no past, no future, no 'now'."

He refilled his teacup, allowing Ascar to interrupt with: "But there *is* time."

Shiu nodded patiently. "Localised, accidental phenomena without overall significance. Processes of time *can* begin over small areas, usually associated with a planet, though not always. They consist of flows or waves of energy travelling from one point to another: small, travelling waves of 'now'. Philosophically it's explained thus: the universe issued from the Supreme as an interplay between the forces of *yin* and *yang* to form a perfect, dead-locked harmonic balance. Occasionally these forces get a little out of balance with one another here and there, and this causes time energy to flow until the balance is redressed. As such a wave proceeds it organises matter into living forms in the process we know as evolution."

"So time is a biological phenomenon, not a universal one?"

"Rather, biology is a consequence of time. Biological systems aren't the only phenomena it can produce. There are – many variations. But life and consciousness can arise in the moving present moment and be carried along with it.

"You can see now why time travel is comparatively easy," Shiu went on. "We merely have to detach a fragment of the travelling 'now-wave' and move it about the real static world of non-time. It comes away quite easily, because it's local energy, not part of a cosmic schema."

"Yes, and we've found that you need a living presence to make a time machine work," Ascar agreed. "That would follow, too."

"Only because your machinery is primitive. In Retort City we can dispatch inanimate objects through time as well."

"Yes . . . I see. . . ."

Ascar strained to grasp in entirety the vision Shiu Kung-Chien was presenting to him. "So let's put this together," he said with difficulty. "The universe consists of a static four-dimensional matrix —"

"Not four-dimensional," Shiu corrected. "Your whole theories about dimensions are erroneous: there are no dimensions. But if you want to use them as a descriptive tool, that's all right. In that case a six-dimensional matrix would suffice to describe all the possible directions that exist. Time-waves, when they arise, can take any one of these directions – from our point of view, forward, backward, sideways, up, down, inside-out – directions impossible to envisage. But the wave-front always abstracts, as it proceeds, a three-dimensional environment to anyone who is inside it. And it always creates, for an observer trapped in it, a past and a future."

"And the Regression Problem," Ascar reminded him. "What happens to that?"

"There is no Regression Problem. The problem only arises when time is thought of as an absolute factor in the universe. But it's an incidental factor only, a triviality. The universe as a whole

doesn't notice, is indifferent to, time, as well as to all the phenomena such as living creatures which it produces. Therefore there's
no contradiction about before and after, past and future, or the
moving moment. There is, as far as the universe is concerned, no
change; non-time swallows it all up without a whisper."

Considerately, Shiu gave Ascar time to mull this over. The
Earth physicist placed his chin on his hand, gazing at the floor.

"And so this is what's happened to Earth?" he said finally.
"Another time-system has taken root on it, creating another process of evolution . . . but travelling in the reverse direction to
ours. And they're going to collide."

"Correct," affirmed Shiu in a neutral voice.

"I still have difficulty with this. With the idea of time travelling
in reverse, but producing the same effects as our own time. I've
been used to regarding physical laws, such as chemical reac-
tions and the laws of thermodynamics, as working only one way.
The laws of entropy, for instance . . . that would seem to give
time a definite direction irrespective. . . ."

"That's because you're accustomed to looking upon time as an
absolute function. To take the law of entropy – the law that disorder increases with time – the time-wave itself produces this
effect. There are two contrasting modes in every time-wave: first,
the tendency toward increasing disorder, and second, the tendency toward increasing integration, which results in biological
systems. These tendencies are due to the *yin* and *yang* forces
which are present in the time-wave, but battling against one
another instead of harmonising. *Yin* brings the tendency toward
integration, and *yang* brings the tendency toward disorder. When
they cease to war with one another, time dies away."

"But that's not how it's going to be on Earth?"

"No. Your civilisation is most unfortunate, as also is the
civilisation which is going to collide with yours. It will be a violent,
catastrophic conflict between irreconcilable powers – the weirdest,
most fantastic event, perhaps, that can happen in this universe."

"What will happen?"

"Almost certainly the end result will be that time will cease.
The two wave-fronts will cancel one another out in a sort of time
explosion."

"What I really meant was," Ascar said, avoiding Shiu's eye,
"what will it be like for the people on location – caught on the
spot when the wave-fronts came within range of one another?"

"You want to know what it will be like?" Shiu said. "To a certain extent, I can show you."

He rose and walked toward the other side of the laboratory, making for a transparent sphere about eight feet in diameter. "Retort City once suffered a similar incident."

Ascar sprang to his feet and joined him. "And you survived?" he exclaimed.

"It wasn't quite as disastrous as it will be with you," Shiu told him mildly. "For one thing, the angle of approach was small – the entity we encountered was moving obliquely to us through time, not in head-on collision as will be the case with you. For another, we gained an advantage from our situation here in interstellar space. We were forewarned and were able to move ourselves, so that there was no actual physical contact. Nevertheless the wave-fronts *did* interfere with one another, and the effects were extremely unpleasant. It's the closest we've come to annihilation."

He halted before the transparent sphere. "At the time some all-sense tapes were made of the event. Do you have all-sense recording on Earth?"

Dumbly Ascar shook his head.

"As its name implies, it gives a record covering all the senses – all the external senses, and besides that the internal senses as well, such as body feeling, and so on. Where the senses are, the mind is; therefore you won't be able to distinguish the experience from the real thing."

He turned to his guest. "I'll play you one of these sense-tapes if you like. I warn you it will be somewhat disturbing."

"Yes, yes," Ascar said eagerly. "I want to know what happens."

Shiu nodded, his expression withdrawn and unreadable, and directed Ascar to enter the sphere by a narrow hatchway which closed up behind him. Once Ascar could no longer see him he smiled faintly to himself. He was unexpectedly pleased with the Terran visitor; despite his barbarian origin he was proving to be an apt pupil.

From within, the walls of the sphere were opaque. There was a dim light, by which Ascar saw a chair fixed to the floor. He sat on it, and as he did so the light went out, leaving him in pitch-darkness.

For a few moments nothing happened. Then light sprang into being again. But he was no longer in the glass sphere. He was sitting in a similar chair in a typically light, airy room in Retort City. The air carried a mingle of faint scents, and from somewhere came strains of the jangly, hesitating music that was popular here.

He stared at the room's fittings for a while before he began to see that there was something odd about his surroundings. The proportions of the room were wrong, and seemed to become more wrong by the second. The angles of the walls, floor and ceiling . . . they didn't add up, he realised; they were an impossible combination, as if space itself were altering its geometry.

The music, in the middle of a complicated progression, became stuck on one chord which elongated and prolonged itself, wailing and wavering, unable to escape its imprisonment in one moment of time.

Ascar watched with bulging eyes as a slim vase left the shelf on which it stood and moved through the air on an intricate orbit. This in itself was not so amazing; but the vase itself was deforming, going through a variegated procession of shapes. Finally Ascar found that he was looking at the vase transformed into a *four-dimensional object* – something akin to a klein bottle, impossible in three-dimensional space, with no inside, no outside, but comprising a continuous series of curved surfaces all running into one another.

He felt stunned to think that not only could he visualise such a figure but he was *actually seeing it.*

Everything else in the room began to deform in the same way. Alarmed, Ascar tried to rise from his chair – but couldn't. Dimly, he tried to remind himself that he was being subjected to a recording, not an actual event; presumably the sense-tapes inhibited the power of movement in some way. Soon he stopped even trying, for the deformations, quite horribly, were acting on him, too.

Ascar let out a long, howling scream. Pain — Pain — Pain.

Then the room collapsed and was replaced by something indefinable. Ascar became aware of his nervous system as a skein,

108

or network, floating like a rambling cloud, without tangible form, drifting through a multidimensional maze. Nothing was recognisable any more, and neither was there any proper sense of time. But his nerves, perhaps because the intruding time field had compromised their chemical functioning, were signalling pain: agonising, sharp, irresistible.

And into his consciousness was intruding something that, it seemed, was imminently going to end that consciousness. *Thump, thump, thump,* it went, like a living heart, or like a hammer that had his soul on the anvil.

Around him, his surroundings seemed to crystallise into some sort of form for a few moments. He saw more than the room in which he'd been seated: he saw a whole section of Retort City, deformed into bizarre non-Euclidean geometries so that its walls were no longer impediments to vision. Trapped in that nightmare were thousands of people, themselves transformed beyond semblance of humanity, like flies in a sticky jungle of spider-web: protruding through walls, floors and ceilings, combined with pieces of furniture, broken up into fragments of bodies still connected by long threads that were drawn-out nerves.

Then the city was on the move again, folding, distorting, sliding together like some shapeless, living monster from the ocean's ooze.

Shiu Kung-Chien, watching a monitor of the tapes on a small screen set into the sphere's pedestal, chose that moment to cut the playback, before there was any risk of Ascar suffering psychosomatic damage.

He switched on the sphere's internal light and opened the hatch. Leard Ascar staggered forth, his face haggard and his breath coming in gasps.

"I think that will do," Shiu said mildly. "It gets worse, but we don't want to make a psychiatric case out of you."

"It gets worse?"

"Yes. What you experienced were the effects of the initial approach of an alien time field. By the time it was all over our population had actually been decimated. We might not have got off so lightly, had the Oblique Intelligence itself, being also able to manipulate time, not taken steps to alter its direction."

Ascar hung onto the edge of the hatch. "And this is what it's going to be like in Earth?" he wanted to know.

"Oh, on your planet it will be incomparably worse than anything that happened here. Ours was merely a glancing blow, scarcely more than a close passage. What it will be like for you is scarcely conceivable."

"Holy Mother Earth!" whispered Ascar hoarsely.

10.

Hwen Wu's cabinet ministers sat gazing impassively at the two Earthmen, their expressions mild, faintly supercilious. Rond Heshke found this detached look, which the people of Retort City invariably wore, somewhat unnerving. It was as if they weren't really interested in one at all.

"So you understand, I hope, the situation that faces your planet," Hwen Wu said calmly, conversationally, as though he were discussing how they might spend an idle hour or two. "We in Retort City have been aware of it for some months, ever since Shiu Kung-Chien made a chance survey in that direction. That's why we put a space-timeship in orbit around Earth to make detailed observations."

"How come our people never detected your ship?" Ascar asked sharply. "Our tracking stations keep watch on the whole solar system."

"Its orbit was elliptical in time, I believe," the Prime Minister told him, "swinging not only around the planet in space but also from the past to the future and from the future to the past. Your surveillance stations would never have picked it up."

"Ingenious," Ascar murmured to himself.

Hwen Wu continued. "Recently we decided to offer Earth what assistance we could afford. For this, since we're racially unacceptable to your ideology, we needed emissaries your government would trust. That explains your presence here in Retort City: our observers watched your tragic journey through non-time and decided you'd be most suitable. You're both eminent personages on Earth and were already to some degree acquainted with the facts."

"What is it you want us to do?" asked Heshke.

"Merely return to Earth and make representations to your government, advising them of the facts and the help we can offer."

111

"And just what form of help is that?" Ascar demanded, frowning doubtfully.

"The only solution for your civilisation lies in the style of life we've adopted," Hwen Wu said. "By that, I mean a life in space, lived in artificial cities. You must get off the planet before the disaster strikes."

Heshke was aghast. "But that's practically impossible. We can't possible take *everyone* off!"

"Not everyone, true. But we'll be able to help you. Our productive facilities are as great, if not greater, than those of your civilisation. We're able to put our Production Retort – the lower half of our city – through cycles of time, so that it can go through several production periods where an Earth factory would go through only one."

"We'll show you how to construct your space cities," an aged, venerable minister put in, "and add our resources to your own."

Hwen Wu nodded in agreement. "The two time systems won't meet for generations yet. We should be able to establish, perhaps, two hundred million people in space. It might even be greater, but" – he waved a hand negligently – "we'll also be making a similar offer to the civilisation which unhappily is to be in collision with yours, and probably the Production Retort will be working to capacity."

"Two hundred million people – that's only a fraction of the population of Earth."

"But enough to allow your culture to continue, surely. We're motivated, in part, by a desire not to see interesting cultures destroyed needlessly."

"Interesting cultures?" echoed Heshke in bewilderment. "But do you not realise that by the norms of *my* culture *you* are biological perversions? Freaks? And should be exterminated? And you want to help *us*?"

"Your religious beliefs don't influence us in any way," replied Hwen Wu in his usual cold but cultivated voice. "We're swayed by reason, by what's possible, but not, I hope, by passion."

"It won't work," said Ascar, an acid, final note in his voice. "The Titanium Legions just won't hear of it. The Earth is a goddess to them. They won't desert her in any circumstances."

"I fear Ascar may be right," Heshke sighed. "Is there no other way? You're masters of time: can't you do something to prevent the collision from taking place at all?"

"You ask the impossible," Hwen Wu said. "We're not masters to that degree! We're able to control a time field large enough to cover this city, yes – but one so large and powerful as either of the two on Earth? It would be like trying to move the Earth itself. It that not so, Leard Ascar?"

"So Shiu Kung-Chien informs me," complied Ascar dully.

"And what if my government *does* refuse?" Heshke asked.

Hwen Wu gave a small, delicate shrug. "Then that's their affair. We'll take no further interest."

He rose to his feet and waved his hand, signalling a cybernetic servitor. The machine rolled to a flimsy screen door and slid the panel aside.

"You won't return to Earth alone," Hwen Wu said. "One of our people will come with you, naturally, as our liaison. If your mission is successful he'll stay on Earth to help to coordinate our joint efforts."

Into the room walked Hueh Su-Mueng.

Heshke reclined on a low couch, wiping his brow with ice cubes wrapped in a cloth. His head ached and he was tired. He needed a long rest; he was scheduled to leave for Earth tomorrow.

Tomorrow and tomorrow and tomorrow. . . .

Time's illusion.

Nearby was a decanter of a light, peach-tinted wine, of which Heshke had taken a draught. It was refreshing on the tongue and had an invigorating effect, but he was in no mood to drink any more of it.

Ascar, however, sloshed it back with gusto. "I think it's very bad of you," Heshke reproved him, "to back out at a time like this. In spite of your past actions, which have been awful enough, I'd have expected you to show a greater sense of responsibility, in the circumstances."

The physicist had announced that he wouldn't be returning to Earth with Heshke. Shiu Kung-Chien had accepted him as a pupil; he washed his hands of Retort City's entire scheme for the sake of an academic career under the great master.

He guffawed to hear Heshke's protest. "You know what the Titans are like," he said. "The whole enterprise is a lost cause. I'm too old to back any more lost causes – you're quite capable of conducting the fiasco by yourself."

Perhaps he's right, Heshke thought to himself. I've suffered enough mental upheavals myself lately. Someone as unbalanced as Ascar probably *would* react by turning his back on everything, his whole race, his whole planet.

Not that Heshke could count himself as a racist any more. As an archaeologist, he had taken good care to delve into Retort City's version of Earth history. Theirs wasn't archaeological inference, it was recorded fact. And the fact was that there never had been an alien interventionist invasion, never had been such a thing as True Man. Human civilisation had risen and fallen into barbarism again and again of its own accord, that being its pattern. The elders of Retort City claimed that theirs was the only system that wasn't subject to that pattern, the only one that could preserve itself for millennium after millennium. As for the deviant subspecies, Heshke knew now that Blare Oblomot's version of their arising had been the correct one. It was a natural tendency for species to radiate into diverse subspecies. Usually, when there were global communications, so much interbreeding took place that the different strains all merged. But some time ago, after one particularly violent collapse, geographical groups of men had been isolated from one another for a lengthy period. The natural mutation rate had been accelerated by radiation left over from a series of nuclear wars, and they had evolved into distinct races.

And the subspecies to which Heshke belonged – known in Titan racial science as True Man – didn't particularly resemble the *homo sapiens* that had existed, say, thirty thousand years ago, any more than the others did. It was simply the one that had come out on top.

"I wonder if Hwen Wu's scheme extends to rescuing the dev cultures, too," he mused, dropping his futile attempt to make Ascar feel ashamed of himself. "Did you know there's an organised underground on Earth, opposed to the Titans and trying to help the devs?"

Ascar grimaced. "Yeah, I know of them. The Panhumanic League. A bunch of nuts."

"Well, I suppose the devs are pretty well beyond any kind of help now, anyway." He put down the ice and wiped his brow with a towel. "Tell me, Leard, what do you think of our hosts?"

"What do I think of them? Why, they're brilliant, of course!"

"I'm not sure I like them. There's something cold about them. Something too logical, too sophisticated. They're effete, over-cultured . . . without any real compassion."

Ascar grunted. "You sound like a Titan education tape."

"Perhaps. But have you learned how their social system works? How they give up their children to be brought up as workers and technicians?" Heshke could remember the horror and revulsion he had felt when the system had first been explained to him. The two retorts were phased differently in time. The children of the Leisure Retort, taken from their parents at birth, were passed back twenty-five years in time. They grew up and usually, at the age of about twenty-five years, had children of their own . . . which were passed to the Leisure Retort. People gave up their babies and *on the same day* received a baby in return . . . their grandchild.

"I think it's fascinating," Ascar said, a rare smile coming to his features. "They play all kinds of tricks with time. They oscillate the Production Retort through phases, sending it on cycles – not just forward and backward but sideways in some way, in other dimensions. . . . You know what this means? Here in the Leisure Retort you can order something that takes six months to make, and it's delivered five minutes later. Shiu Kung-Chien does it all the time. Beautiful! "

"Beautiful if you're Shiu Kung-Chien!" Heshke said angrily. "What if you're the man who has to spend his life satisfying these people's whims?" It all made the Titans' plans for humanity – True Man, anyway – seem just and compassionate, he thought. At least the Titans believed in a kind of rough democracy. And they believed in culture – even for the workers.

"Oh, they do all right," Ascar said vaguely. "They're looked after, they're happy. And anyway we're not down there, so what are you worried about?"

"If you don't mind," Heshke said wearily, defeated by the man's single-minded narrowness, "I'd like to get some sleep. We're starting early in the morning."

"Oh. Well, don't say I didn't warn you." Ascar backed out of the room. He didn't bother to say good-bye.

11.

Outside the big room's windows the murmur of traffic rose up from the busy street below.

By the general standard of Titan appointments the room – Limnich's own private office – was not luxurious, almost drab. The Planetary Leader was renowned for his modest life-style, his retiring habits. His office was not even situated in Bupolbloc, but in a two-hundred-year-old building outside the newly-built administrative sector of the city. Here he kept his collection of skulls, his library of racist lore, and his other collections and paraphernalia.

In the past few days the office had been the scene of an unaccustomed surge of activity, disturbing the contemplative silences of its dark, varnished wood and its soft-piled carpets. Limnich himself confessed to being shaken to the core; there was no time for a dignified convention at the great castle. Everything had to be done now, on the spot. His office had become the nerve centre of the planet as he reorganised the Titanium Legions for the unprecedented struggle ahead.

Many of the old generals had gone, either retired or shunted to administrative roles requiring less initiative. Limnich had replaced them with younger men who had fresh, brilliant minds and newly-minted fervour – men like Colonel Brask (until the onset of the emergency he had been Captain Brask) who had been associated with the time project from the beginning. These were the type who now worked at the centre of things, preparing a colossal Armageddon in time.

Brask was with him now. On a wall screen behind Limnich's desk he taped a time map that had been drawn up to show the advance of the alien time-system on their own. The map was a moving one, dramatically demonstrating the speed of approach and the estimated point of impact.

Limnich's bones felt chill as he looked with awe upon that advancing wall of time. "So we have nearly two centuries?" he said.

"To total impact, yes," Brask told him. "But the effects will be felt far before then. Our knowledge at this stage is still incomplete, but we estimate that the interference effects will become noticeable in about fifty years. After a hundred years, we aren't sure what our operational status will be. Perhaps zero."

"Thank God we discovered the truth in time!"

He turned from the screen toward Brask. In the room's grey light the younger man's oddly deformed eyelid looked almost grotesque. In a less talented man that eyelid would have excluded him from the Titanium Legions altogether, but the exhaustive genealogical investigation every applicant underwent had shown the defect to have no genetic origin, and Limnich had let it pass.

In spite of his own fanaticism in that area, he did sometimes exercise leniency if there was an advantage in it. There was actually an officer in the new Command Team – a Colonel Yedrasch – who was part Lorene. But he was a ferocious fighter for True Man, even more so, it seemed, because of his knowledge of his mixed nature, and his services to the race were of such a high order that Limnich had decided (and the World President agreed with him) that he couldn't be dispensed with. Thus, instead of liquidation, Yedrasch had merely undergone a vasectomy to ensure that he could not defile the future blood of True Man.

An oak-panelled door opened. "Colonel Hutt is here, Leader," Limnich's secretary told him.

Limnich nodded curtly. Titan-Colonel Hutt entered. Both men gave the hooked-arm salute, then Limnich sat down.

"About the question of public information, Leader. . . ."

Limnich nodded again. "I've made a decision. The average man's intelligence is too limited to be able to comprehend the whole truth all at once. The public announcements are to give a more restricted idea of the nature of time: they will speak of an attack from the future, where the alien interventionists have established their second attempt to settle the Earth."

"In other words, the public is to understand the matter as we ourselves did until recently," Brask added. "Later, when they've been further educated, the full facts can be made clear."

"I understand," Titan-Colonel Hutt said.

"There's one other point," Limnich resumed. "The emergency,

the greatest that has ever faced mankind, will entail a big political crisis. All political work must be intensified. Dissident groups must be totally nullified. To this end, I order you to apprise the Panhumanic League of *all* the facts at our disposal, through our secret contacts."

"*All* the facts, Leader?" Hutt echoed in dismay. "But why?"

"What better way could there be of pulling the ground from under their feet?" Limnich said, his face fish-cold and unsmiling. "It's a certain bet that the larger part of the League will defect and come over to us, once they know the truth."

A look of dawning realisation came over the other's face. "Correct, Leader. That is so." He was reassured to see that the old fox had not lost his grip, that Limnich's sense of manoeuvre was as subtle as ever.

Limnich, for his part, fought to snatch his mind back from the edge of madness. His brain filled yet again with a dreadful, incomprehensible vision of two onrushing time-systems encountering one another. He hadn't even begun to think how this looked from the aspect of the Earth Mother, a deity in whom he believed without question. He didn't even want to think about it.

"Thank God we discovered the truth in time!" he repeated in a low voice. But had that done any good? Could *anything* save them?

The Approach to the future-Earth aliens was necessarily more incautious than that planned for the Titans. The task before Wang Yat-Sen and Li Li-San, the two young philosophers selected for it by the Prime Minister, was a delicate one.

Firstly they had to convince the lemur-like creatures that they were *not* from the civilisation that was threatening them. This was no easy matter, since the aliens were, naturally, insensitive to fine differences of physique. But already the previous expedition had decoded the aliens' language (in fact, several languages) from electromagnetic transmissions and had prepared language-course tapes. Consequently Wang Yat-Sen and Li Li-San were fairly competent in the hesitant, chittering tongue, though their pronunciation brought them barely within the bounds of intelligibility.

Eventually the aliens were, it seemed, persuaded, and the two young men were taken from the prison-hospital (actually a biological research station) where they had been kept with the other human prisoners (and what they had seen being done to those prisoners was most distasteful).

Now they sat in a conically shaped room of bare stone. The aliens seemed to go in for bare stone, as well as for conical shapes in building, and all the doors were triangular, too low for a man to go through without bending. The furnishings of the room were sparse, made of square-cut unpolished timber and board. The aliens' technological achievements were not matched by any interest in interior decoration.

But the two individuals who faced the young men across the rough plank table were among the highest authorities in their society. Wang Yat-Sen gazed at them calmly, fascinated as usual by their nervous sensitivity. Anything was enough to set their fragile bodies to quivering, and their fine nose-whiskers to twitching and vibrating.

"And why should you make us this offer?" chittered one. "Why should you go to such lengths to help us? How are we to know that this is not some devious trick?"

"To take your points one at a time," Li Li-San answered, "our readiness to give assistance merely demonstrates the good regard of one intelligent species for another. Your second point: guarantees of good faith can be arranged. Our offer applies also to the other, human civilisation. If you both agree, then you'll be co-operating with one another instead of fighting."

"We will, if you wish, take your ambassadors to our ISS," Wang Yat-Sen put in equably. "Then they'll see for themselves."

The lemur-creature ignored this last. "You expect us to retreat from the enemy? To abandon our planet?" he said, his vowel-sounds indicating considerable passion. His limbs were trembling visibly, like those of a mortally wounded animal. "It's *our* planet, ours since the beginning of time. We'll defend it to the last."

The other lemur-creature joined in. "Never do we retreat from an enemy. A few days ago they – your biological cousins – launched an attack upon two of our large cities, using weapons, which, judging by the intensity of the energy produced, relied upon the fusion of light atomic nuclei. Our cities were utterly destroyed and there is radioactive waste for distances all around. But we'll strike back! We'll strike back!"

Both men from Retort City, brought up to regard everything in a detached and clinical manner, were puzzled. "But surely you realise that your emotional attitude toward your historical habitat is inappropriate in the current situation," Wang Yat-Sen put forward. "Your 'enemy', as you put it, is merely reacting in the same manner, and to attacks you've made on him. Evacuation is the only hope for either of you."

"We don't accept that it's the only hope," chittered the lemur-leader shrilly. "We know that enemy life-forms lie in our future, and that if they continue to exist, we'll perish. Therefore – we'll deal with it!"

"But how?" Li Li-San asked simply.

"We're developing viruses destructive to all life in the enemy *biota*," the lemur said. "We'll sow these viruses on a massive scale. By the time our time-system reaches the projected collision point, all trace of life in the enemy biosphere will be gone. There'll be nothing to obstruct the passage of our own time-wave."

Glancing at one another, Wang Yat-Sen and Li Li-San saw from each other's expressions that they both concluded that their mission had failed. They stood up.

"Apparently your decisions are not guided by rationality and we take it that you reject our offer," Wang Yat-Sen announced, still using the "friendly" mode of speech. "There is, then, nothing more to detain us. With your permission we'll call down our space lighter and return to our people."

"Oh, no!" squeaked the lemur. "You're not returning anywhere with information that can be used against us. You're of the same race as our enemy – so back to the bio-research unit with you!"

And so the two young men were transported back to the Biological Warfare Station, which they were never to leave.

As soon as he entered the cellar complex, Sobrie Oblomot knew that something was extraordinarily wrong.

This time the Council meeting was to have been in Sannan, Sobrie's native city. These ancient cellars were completely unknown to the authorities; they had been sealed over during a rebuilding programme years ago. The hidden entrances were few, and known only to trusted League agents.

A printing press was run down here and Sobrie was struck, first of all, by its silence: never before had he known it not to be clattering away. And yet the place was gripped by a sense of feverish excitement: the whitewashed brick walls almost visibly shone with it.

Groups of people stood around, talking with agitation. A small thin man wormed his way between them and rushed up to Sobrie.

"Oblomot! You're here!"

"What's going on?" Sobrie said with deference.

"If I were you," the small man said in a low voice, "I'd get out
– now. And take your girl friend with you. Because —"

But he was interrupted by the convener, who appeared suddenly at Sobrie's elbow. "So you made it, Oblomot. You're late.
We'd thought you might already have heard."

"Heard what?"

"The news is all over the networks. Right across the globe. It
looks like the end."

To Sobrie's bewildered demands for enlightenment he responded
merely by guiding him across the floor and through a low archway. A door opened, closed again once Sobrie was through.

The Panhumanic Council was sitting. Eyes turned to regard
Sobrie sombrely. They weren't all there, he realised; about a third
were missing.

With a start, he noticed that one of the faces was unfamiliar.
It was the anonymous member, sitting for the first time without
mask or voice modifier!

What could have brought about such a change in policy?
Curiously he studied the face. It was striking: a strong, clear
face with much character, fair-skinned, blue-eyed, flaxen-haired –
it was such a perfect example of the Titan ideal that its owner
just *had* to be a Titan. That was it: he was a high-ranking,
famous Titan officer who also happened to be secretly a member
of the Panhumanic League. Sobrie vaguely recalled seeing his
face, now. He was one of the idolised heroes who appeared on the
covers of glossy magazines, on vidcast pageants and the like.

"Sit down, Oblomot," the Chairman said, his voice heavy with
strain.

"Incredible!" was Sobrie's reaction. "It's just unbelievable."

"Unbelievable but true."

"Can we be sure? Suppose it's just another Titan story? An
invention?"

"It's true enough," the once-anonymous member said. "It comes
from two sources. The Titans have intentionally passed the information to the League, through contacts they have. But I'm able
to confirm it independently, through my position in the Legions.
The consternation among ourselves is nothing compared with
what's going on there, I assure you."

Without the voice modifier the Titan's voice was strong and resonant, mature but somehow still youthful. "I don't really understand all that scientific stuff you just read out," Sobrie said to the Chairman. "But is that literally true – that we'll all be annihilated? By an alien . . . time-wave . . . from the future?"

"Not only us, but all life on Earth. Unless we can find a way to stop it."

"And where does that leave us – the League?"

"That's what we were discussing before you came in," the Chairman told him after a heavy pause. "It's no good denying that what we thought was Titan paranoia has, in the event, been vindicated. We *are* threatened by an alien power, albeit in a form so weird and overwhelming that the Titans could never have foreseen it. Our own objectives now seem futile, not to say insignificant. . . ."

"The League must disband itself voluntarily and go over to the Titans," a voice said. "That will happen anyway, among the greater part of our membership."

"Those of us who failed to attend this meeting doubtless have already taken that step," the Chairman added.

Sobrie was shocked by this talk. To talk of joining forces with the hated Titans! To abandon the age-old goal of racial equality!

"But we *can't* do that!" he protested. "We have a sacred mission!"

The Titan spoke. "As I see it, there is very little choice. It's not a matter of saving threatened subspecies any more. It's a matter of the survival of mankind. I, who have lived with the Titans all my life, and have always hated them, now see that only they can save us. They're the only hope for humanity: from now on I'll be a loyal Titan officer."

Sobrie's wasn't the only voice to express dismay at the way things were going. Two others broke in together, making angry denunciations of this betrayal of their ideals.

Sobrie added his own accusations. "And what of the dev subspecies?" he flared. "The Amhraks, the Urukuri and the others? Are they to be abandoned?"

"Regrettably, they must go by the board," the unmasked Titan said evenly. "They're too trivial to deserve our attention in a crisis of such proportions as this. It's humanity, not any particular subspecies, that's at stake."

Voices rose in violent argument. And faces that had long grown

122

hard in a life of continuous plotting began to show their determination, one way or the other.

Sobrie was not sure how, or when, shooting broke out. Guns seemed to appear in several hands at once. A bullet caught the Titan in the chest and he went down, slumping against the table, his handsome, clean-cut face sagging in extreme nervous shock. Shots exploded deafeningly. The Chairman, even as he squeezed the trigger, was hit in the shoulder and spun around with a snarl of pain.

Somewhat belatedly Sobrie produced his own gun, ducking below the level of the table, only to see that all the voices that had been added to his side of the argument had been silenced, their owners dead.

He ripped open his shirt, plunged his hand inside, and slowly rose.

Guns were trained on him. He took his hand from his shirt and held up the s-grenade he had taken from his body-pouch.

"Don't move, anyone," he said in a strained voice, "or we all get it."

Step by step he backed to the door, their eyes watching him blankly. In seconds he had reached it, flung it open and then was racing through the cavernous cellars.

White faces, shocked by the sound of gunfire, stared at him, their mouths black holes. He waved the gun and shoved people aside, strangely aware that no pursuit was, as yet, being organised. No more than twenty seconds passed before he had reached the nearest exit. He plunged into it, up the dank tunnel, pounding along it for yard after yard.

The tunnel ended in a concealed door which opened on to yet another cellar beneath a disused warehouse. Sobrie presently emerged in a side street in an outlying district of Sannan. He hurried from the spot to more populated streets, and stopped at the first vidbooth.

Layella's face came up on the screen. Her eyes widened at the sight of him.

"Hello. What is it?"

"Layella, get out of the apartment right away."

Alarm showed on her features. "What?"

"Get out of there *this minute*. Don't wait to take anything – just as much money as you can snatch up." He thought for a moment. "Meet me under the clock in Kotsin Square. Have you

123

got that?"

Her face became pale, but calm. "Yes."

"Right." He killed the screen, and a moment later was pacing the busy street, his mind racing, trying to figure the situation from all angles. They'd have to leave Sannan, and quickly. They could go – my God, where? Everything was in turmoil. Already the networks would be breaking open; there'd be almost nothing left.

He took a tubeway and came up some distance from Kotsin Square. Making a rough calculation of how long it would take Layella to get there, he walked slowly the rest of the way. When he arrived she was already waiting, looking nervous and fidgety, dressed in a drab brown coat.

"Where are we going?" she asked, looking at him with round, Amhrak eyes.

"We'll go to Jorb Gandatt," he said. "He'll help us." Some of the League was bound to survive, he told himself. There were bound to be some diehards, like himself and Jorb, who wouldn't surrender. Enough would pull through so that some kind of organisation remained.

He felt sure that Jorb was trustworthy and that he'd be able to help them. The Sannan circuit (his own circuit, he thought ruefully, the one he commanded) would be entirely blown, but Jorb didn't belong to it; he was one of Sobrie's contacts with the outside. He might be able to tell them where to go to be safe.

She took his arm as they crossed the square. At first he didn't notice that the entrance to Kotsin Square seemed a little crowded, or the grey van, without any insignia or designation, that was parked unobtrusively to one side of the square. But just before they entered the throng they were both taken roughly by the arms and propelled toward the vehicle.

The back of the van was open. Inside sat a pudgy little man who had been scanning the square through a set of periscopes. Sobrie realised, with a sudden jump of his heart, that they'd fallen into one of those Titan devices one heard about but never met: a roving racial street-check. And the pudgy man was that half-legendary figure, the dev expert: one who could tell a dev or a part-dev at a glance.

The dev expert looked Layella up and down as though she were something dirty. "She's one all right," he said in an acid, slightly nasal voice. "I don't know how she's got away with it so long."

Sobrie gave a strangled cry. Whether he'd have had the nerve to use his s-grenade, thus killing Layella too, he'd never know. Because two plainclothes Titans held him with arms outspread, while one reached under his shirt and yanked out the deadly device.

"Interesting," murmured Limnich. "And Leard Ascar is still out there, you say?"

"Yes, Leader," said Heshke.

"Hmm. Of course, we've always known there was a possibility of human settlements existing out among the stars – some of them perhaps dev. There are indications of interstellar flight in the records of the Pundish Aeon – but you know that, of course, Citizen Heshke."

"Yes, Leader," Heshke said again, slightly embarrassed. Planetary Leader Limnich was, as Heshke had found during meetings with him earlier in his career, obsessive about anything bearing on the history of True Man. His knowledge of archaeological detail came close to challenging Heshke's own.

Heshke faced Limnich across the latter's massive desk, and was spoken to respectfully by him. Hueh Su-Mueng was also present, but was forced to sit in the corner, flanked by two guards. Planetary Leader Limnich cast him a disdainful glance every now and then, plainly disliking to have the dev in his office.

"And what do *you* make of this plan of theirs, Heshke? What's their ulterior motive?"

"I sincerely believe they have no ulterior motive, Leader," Heshke told him frankly. "They evidently have no designs on Earth, indeed no direct interest in our planet at all. Strange though it may seem, they're prompted simply by the urge to help a neighbour in distress."

"The fiendishly clever Chink," Limnich muttered audibly, nodding to himself as if with some inner satisfaction.

"Yes, I've heard the phrase before," Heshke said stiffly.

Behind Limnich stood Colonel Brask, looking on the scene much as Heshke recalled him doing on that day in Titan-Major Brourne's office. The looks he gave Hueh, however, displayed undisguised loathing.

"And how did you find it, living with . . . the Chinks?" Brask asked him.

Heshke squirmed uncomfortably. "They are . . . not like us," he admitted.

"Indeed not."

"I was impressed, however, by how much they could help us," Heshke added.

Brask gave a smile of wintry sarcasm, and Limnich replied: "Whatever their intentions were, their scheme has come unstuck this time. Surely you're aware, Citizen Heshke, that we'll never give up our efforts to hold Earth for True Man. The son doesn't desert his mother, even to save his own life – and no matter how dire the peril to them both. We're building up our power to defend our birthright. That defence will be total – desperate, perhaps – but overwhelming. Titan-Colonel Brask here, as it happens, is in charge of the formation of the Titanium Legions of Kronos, named after the ancient god of time, that will enable us – already are enabling us – to strike across the centuries. *He* can tell you that we're not beaten yet."

"But you know the nature of the catastrophe that's coming!" Heshke exploded. "It's a *natural* catastrophe, not due to any living enemy. How are you going to deal with *that?*"

"We already have a plan," Brask told him loftily.

"And what's that? I'm fascinated!" Despite being in the presence of such charismatically high rank, Heshke couldn't keep the sarcasm out of his voice.

"Our aim is to effect the total annihilation of the enemy's biosphere. By means of a massive nuclear attack we'll eradicate all life, so that not a microbe remains. Their time-system is associated with the existence of life: consequently, by removing that time-wave, which will die with the death of alien life, we remove the impediment to our own existence."

Heshke twisted around to look questioningly at Hueh Su-Mueng. But the Retort City technician merely shrugged. He turned back to Brask.

"If you're letting off thousands of fusion explosions —"

"Hundreds of thousands," Brask interrupted tonelessly.

"— if you're doing that four centuries in the future, what happens when *our* time reaches that point? Aren't we going to be headed into all those explosions?"

Brask smiled faintly. "That's one of the peculiar things about time. By the 'time' we get there the effects will have died away – provided we *do* succeed in cancelling out the enemy time-front. If we don't, it won't matter anyway." Noting Heshke's incomprehension, he added: "I know it sounds odd, but that's how

126

time works, apparently."

Heshke looked again at Hueh, who nodded. "He's quite right — *provided* the reversed time-system were to be destroyed."

"Can you now doubt our determination?" Limnich said in his low, fruity voice. "The coming struggle may be the acme of our glory. Let all who come against us know—" He clenched his fists spasmodically, and Heshke thought he actually saw him, as in fact Limnich had done many times, draw himself back from the edge of madness.

Are we an insane race? Heshke wondered darkly. Perhaps so. Perhaps it's good that all is lost. And, in those very thoughts, he thought he detected then the emergence of the death-wish that Blare Oblomot had once claimed pervaded Titan mentality.

"Thank you for seeing us, Planetary Leader," he said humbly.

"Your adventure has been so extraordinary that I could do no less," Limnich responded with a touch of graciousness. He rang a little gold bell that lay on his desk. "Escort these two back to Bupolbloc," he ordered to the extra guards who came in.

In the subterranean levels of Bupolbloc, as Heshke and Hueh were being taken to their adjacent cells, the archaeologist suddenly pulled up short. Coming along the corridor, also under escort, was someone who, after a momentary start of false recognition, he realised was a person he had met but once: Blare Oblomot's brother, Sobrie.

"Oblomot!" he exclaimed.

The other looked at him for a moment, and then smiled bleakly. Their guards made to goad both of them along, but Heshke turned angrily. "I demand to be allowed to talk to this man! I'm not exactly a prisoner, you know!"

"True," said one of the guards indifferently. "Citizen Heshke is in custodial detention only. And he has the ear of the Planetary Leader."

The guards eyed one another for a moment, and then one of them pushed open a door. "In here." And because they didn't want to split the escort, Hueh Su-Mueng was prodded inside too. The guards stood by the door, eyeing their wards, swinging their batons.

Heshke found it easy to ignore them. After some diffidence he explained how he had seen Blare die, but Sobrie merely nodded dismally: he already knew.

In a rush of words Sobrie told him everything that had hap-

127

pened: his involvement with the Panhumanic League, his part-Amhrak girl friend, their arrest and how they'd been brought here to Bupolbloc in Pradna.

"They're trying to make a deal with me," he finished bitterly. "They want to mop up the Panhumanic League once and for all. If I put the finger on enough League members who haven't so far defected they'll let Layella live on the Amhrak reservation instead of . . . putting her down like a dog."

"Could you do that?"

"I could, but . . . oh, God. . . ."

Heshke gave a sad sigh. "Well, at least they show a *trace* of civilised conduct," he said gently. "They could have used third degree."

Sobrie looked at him, startled, and then laughed incredulously. "You don't think they have scruples, do you? It's a matter of time, that's all! They're so busy now that the torture facilities at Bupolbloc Two are being overworked. They don't want to wait while I stand in line!"

One other item of deference Heshke had wrung from the Titans was that he and Hueh were in connected cells, so that they could talk to one another. They held a brief conversation after leaving Sobrie Oblomot.

"I feel sorry for them both," Heshke said. "They're in a hopeless position . . . the Titans will do just what they like with them. This is an evil world, Su-Mueng."

"All worlds have their evils," Su-Mueng observed.

"Perhaps. At any rate, I'm too old for the kind of role I've been expected to play lately. I've done what I can; now I just want to be left alone." Heshke was lying on his pallet. He closed his eyes.

"This plan your friends have won't work," Su-Mueng told him. "They make a basic mistake: the time-wave isn't dependent on organic life, it's the other way around. Biological organisation is a by-product of a time-system, not a cause of it."

"So?"

"It will make no difference if they destroy an entire biosphere: the time-wave will come rolling on just the same."

"Just so," said Heshke faintly. "What can I do about it?"

Moments later he was asleep.

128

Although it was late into the night, Limnich was still at his desk, poring over the genealogical charts of Titan officers who had come under suspicion. Racial vigilance within Earth's elite force was something in which he took a personal interest.

Outside, the murmur of traffic had lapsed into silence, broken only by the drone of an occasional car, and all was quiet. But suddenly Limnich jerked bolt upright and gasped with shock.

There, standing before him in the half-darkened office, was the dev Chink Heshke had brought back with him from space.

Limnich wouldn't have believed it possible for anyone to penetrate the building uninvited; the Chink seemed to have materialised out of thin air. He snatched up a pistol that always lay on a shelf under the lip of his desk, and pointed it at the intruder's stomach with trembling fingers.

"How in the Mother's name did you get in here?" he rasped.

"By being fiendishly clever," Su-Mueng said with a smile, remembering Limnich's earlier remark.

In point of fact his entrance had been made without the least difficulty. For while the Titans had made a thorough search of his person, they had failed to find a number of gadgets which had been strapped to his body *in past time*. Phased one minute into the past, these had been quite undetectable. To make one available, Su-Mueng merely brought it forward into the present.

Chief among these gadgets was a compact personal time-displacer, like the larger, clumsier version he had used to escape from the Production Retort. He had phased *himself* one minute back in time, sprung the lock tumblers on the door of his cell, and simply walked out of Bupolbloc. He had made his way here to Limnich's office, walked unseen past guards and secretaries, and once he was in Limnich's presence phased himself back into normative time.

How to explain this to Limnich, to whom his sudden appearance must smack of magic? "I have a device which renders me invisible," he offered casually. "Please don't be alarmed, Planetary Leader – I'm not here to do you harm. I have a proposal to make, which I hope will work to our mutual advantage."

Limnich kept his gun trained on the dev, trying to control the revulsion that being in the presence of the creature caused him. His free hand strayed to the golden bell that would summon help. But then his sense of calculation overcame his natural feelings. He withdrew his hand and leaned back, looking up into the svelte young Chink's repugnantly inhuman face.

"Go on," he purred.

"Your civilisation is in deep trouble, Planetary Leader," Su-Mueng said easily. "Your planned hydrogen bomb attack on the future-Earth aliens may destroy an enemy, but that will be all. The basic problem will remain: hydrogen bombs *won't* wipe out a powerful time-stream."

Limnich listened carefully to his words, and appeared to take them seriously.

"Indeed? Well, we'll have made progress, nevertheless. And we still have fifty years, perhaps a hundred years, in which to deal with the situation. . . ." His words trailed off broodingly, and his eyes left Su-Mueng's face. He gazed down at his desk, apparently forgetting the gun in his hand.

"Let me tell you something of ISS Retort City," Su-Mueng said. "It has a social, system which is inhuman, unjust and cruel. Do you know why I was chosen for this mission to Earth? Because I'm a renegade, an embarrassment to the masters of my city. They were glad of the chance to get rid of me – because I'll do *anything* to change things as they are there."

Limnich gave an explosive grunt. "They get everywhere! "

"Hah?" Su-Mueng inclined his head inquiringly.

"Subversives. Like worms in the woodwork. All societies are riddled with them. But how does this concern me? Be brief; I have much work to do."

"Don't you realise," Su-Mueng said softly, "what an asset Retort City could be to you? Its industrial capacity is enormous: it could double the output of your whole planet. Besides this, you have much to gain from Retort technology. Our control over the forces of time are far in advance of your own." He held up a smooth ovoid object that fitted into the palm of his hand. "How do you think I was able to make myself invisible and enter your office unseen? I'll show you how to invade and occupy Retort City if, in return, you'll wipe out its social system and allow a more equitable one to replace it."

Limnich finally put down his gun. "How could we invade it?" he asked, his eyes bulging behind his round lenses. "I understand it lies some light-years away."

"Not only that, it's removed in time as well. But you have rocket-driven spaceships, do you not? They'll suffice. I'll show your technicians how to make space-time drives for them – I am," he added incidentally, "a fully trained engineer. With perhaps thirty or forty such ships, carrying a few thousand well-armed men, the city could be taken."

The Planetary Leader became deeply thoughtful, considering this remarkable offer from all angles. A feeling of excitement grew in him as he realised the vast benefits that could accrue.

Hueh Su-Mueng's enormous treachery didn't surprise him in the least. The creature was a Chink, following his natural tendencies. Also, Rond Heshke's report on the dev city confirmed his claims.

"Very well, it's agreed," he said abruptly. "You'll have what you ask for – provided things go as you promise."

A look of triumph came suddenly over the dev's face, quickly to be followed by his usual blandness.

"Now that matters have reached this stage, perhaps I might add one more condition?" he said. "Rond Heshke, whom I've come to look upon as a good man, is saddened by the plight of two friends of his who are being held in Bupolbloc: Sobrie Oblomot and Layella Frauk. Instead of having them put to death, allow them to live on the reservation as he hopes for them."

"What? *You* dare to make petty conditions?" Limnich glowered to find himself being dictated to by this subhuman. "Do you think we depend on your goodwill? More of this and I'll simply *torture* cooperation out of you." And the ugly look on his face showed that he meant what he said.

"Remember, we are not as you are," Su-Mueng said coldly. "Perhaps I can withstand torture. And have you not asked yourself why I'm doing all this? I alone of all my people seem to know the meaning of strong human relationships. That's why I feel for the man and the girl in Bupolbloc – they have such a relationship. Such a bond. There was a bond between my father and myself, and he was put to death for it. *That* is why I'm doing this – because I am a son to my father. *You* can understand that, can't you? Your people aren't strangers to these feelings."

Limnich didn't answer immediately. But for the first time the hint of a smile, even of amicability, came to his features.

"Yes," he said sardonically, "I can understand that."

"There's one other small problem," Su-Mueng said with a frown, a few days later.

"And what's that?" Limnich leaned back, strangely at ease.

131

In spite of the physical revulsion he still felt for the Chink (at first he'd been obliged to stifle an impulse to vomit), alongside with that revulsion he found that he derived a perverse pleasure from their dealings together. It was spicy, like having truck with the devil.

"The ship that brought us here is still in orbit around Earth. It would certainly spot our armada."

"Can't we destroy it?"

"Possibly, but it's doubtful. And if we failed, it would return immediately to warn Retort City. By the time *we* got there, we'd find them prepared."

"Then we need to get it out of the way. I suggest you contact the ship and tell it to return to base forthwith."

"They wouldn't go without either myself or Rond Heshke. That would be against all protocol." For once Su-Mueng was at a loss.

"So? Send Heshke," said Limnich impatiently. He didn't like to be upset by such details.

"Apparently he doesn't want to go either."

"Hmm." Limnich pondered. "Can *he* contact this ship?"

"He could if I gave him my communicator."

"Good. Then I'll make him *want* to go. You asked for some friends of his to be sent to a dev reservation, didn't you? Well, they will be – and *he* can join them."

"I don't understand."

The Planetary Leader gave a humourless smile. "The dev reservations are to be closed down within the next few weeks, their inmates liquidated. I'll see that he gets an advance warning. *That* should send him screaming for your orbiting spaceship."

Su-Mueng was uneasy. "I don't like using him as a pawn. . . ."

"All men are pawns," Limnich purred. "When he leaves for the reservation, give him your communicator. Urge him to call the ship to take him off, so he can make a report to your city on his mission. But no hint of what we're really about, mind." He eyed Su-Mueng speculatively. "Maybe you Chinks aren't so clever after all."

12.

The sun was setting on a dusty yellowish landscape broken only by bare, bone-like trees and scattered houses of brick or mud. Rond Heshke, sitting on a verandah backed by a neat bungalow of red brick, looked upon the scene with an unexpected feeling of calm and peace.

Herrick, the Amhrak who owned the bungalow in which Heshke, Sobrie and Layella were staying, came walking toward the building with easy strides, his body swinging characteristically, and Heshke found that even the sudden sight of a full-blooded dev didn't upset his contentment.

At first it had been a tremendous shock to him. He'd been angry and bewildered that he, a respectable citizen with a certificate of racial purity, could be summarily packed off to a dev reservation. His protests had been ignored and he'd gathered that it was because of his friendship with the Oblomot family. After all, Sobrie was being banished too, simply because of his association with Layella. Yes, it had been shocking, at first, to be thrown in with the Amhraks. Had not his experiences with the Chinks already prepared him to some degree, he was sure he might have gone insane.

But now . . . Herrick mounted the steps of the verandah. He was wholly, unstintingly Amhrak. He had the red skin, the compact, round head, the round eyes and the foreign, big-lobed ears. His body, too, had all the disturbing oddness of proportion and of lank, too-easy movement. And it didn't bother Heshke at all. It seemed entirely natural for him to accept Herrick as a charming member of a charming people – all the more so, perhaps, because they represented a now dying culture.

"Hello, Rond," Herrick said with a heavy Amhrak accent. "Is Sobrie in?"

133

Heshke nodded and Herrick swept inside without the usual pleasantries. Heshke continued looking at the receding sun, reflecting on how well the surviving Amhraks had adapted to their circumstances. There were three million of them on this reserve, which measured about two hundred miles across (and yet they had once populated two continents). Most of the land was as Heshke saw it now, arid and useless for cultivation, but the Amhraks had solved that by turning to hydroponics. They had organised themselves into a comprehensive little community, with several small-to-middling towns, and had resurrected a modest amount of industry – all small-scale, just enough for their needs. They were all very much aware that their existence was contingent upon the whim of their conquerors.

While Heshke had known that the Amhraks were technically advanced, he'd always thought this to be due to their copying the inventions of True Man, and it had surprised him, while staying with Herrick, to discover how inventive they were in their own right. Herrick often reminisced about the Amhrak war, when he'd been a young scientist working for the Amhrak's last attempt at defence. He'd been involved, typically, in a project that never reached fruition – a force screen to ward off nuclear warheads.

"The reason why you Whites were able to win," he'd told Heshke (Whites being the Amhrak term for True Man), "is that you have such a capacity for submitting to a central authority, which makes you able to organise yourselves all in one direction. Our social organisation was too loose to be able to stand up to you. Even at the end our energies were being dissipated in countless uncoordinated projects."

"I can't accept that explanation," Heshke had objected "What about the Lorenes?"

"True, the Lorenes had this ability to an ever greater degree. But then, we helped you to defeat the Lorenes. You wouldn't have done it alone."

And to that Heshke had no answer. It was strange, talking to someone whose picture of history didn't follow the Titan version of True Man versus the rest. In official histories past alliances with other subspecies were always played down, and it was never admitted that they could have been important for the outcome. True Man had saved himself unaided, so the text ran, from numerous horrible enemies.

Heshke had soon ceased to battle with contending concepts;

134

it was a relief to be away from it all.

Sometimes he watched Herrick as the Amhrak tinkered, using whatever components he could get his hands on, with an old project of his that had been interrupted by the war: television without any transmitter or camera, only a receiver. Herrick had discovered that by means of a long-range interference technique light-waves could be converted, at a distance, into radio or UHF waves, and these could then be picked up at the control station. In other words it was possible to snatch pictures out of thin air from hundreds of miles away. Heshke would sit with Herrick for hours while he fiddled with his crackling apparatus, occasionally getting a fuzzy, briefly recognisable picture of a mountaintop or a stretch of ocean. There was little control over where the pictures came from, as this apparently depended on the Earth's magnetic field.

The sun slipped down the horizon. Heshke began to feel cold. He got up, stretched himself, and went inside.

Herrick and Sobrie were seated at a table, both looking grim and sober – Sobrie more so, Heshke thought. He looked up as the archaeologist came in.

"Bads news, I'm afraid, Rond." He gestured to Herrick. "We've just heard from Pradna."

"You can still do that?"

Sobrie nodded. "In the past few weeks we've been able to pick up with whatever remnants of the League survived the mass defection to the Titans. Slowly, they're putting themselves together again and thanks to that we still have contacts inside the administration."

He paused. Heshke, in fact, had been impressed by how easily Sobrie had been able to make arrangements for them in Amhrak country. The Panhumanic League's networks apparently extended right into most of the dev reservations; Herrick himself was involved in it.

"Limnich has ordered all reservations to be terminated," Sobrie said quietly. "It's the end of the road for the Amhraks, for all of us."

"We always knew it would happen sooner or later," Herrick said without bitterness. "All we can do is accept it."

Heshke, too, had suspected that this might be coming on.

He reached into his pocket and took out the little communicator Su-Mueng had given him. That young man might have had

135

some intimation of what was impending, too. How else to explain his embarrassed, evasive manner at their last meeting, when he'd urged Heshke to use the communicator and leave Earth?

Su-Mueng had obviously managed to worm his way into the Titans' good books somehow. He'd waved away Heshke's concern for his safety; he had an understanding with Limnich, he'd said vaguely; he was doing important work for him. What an improbable partnership, Heshke told himself.

He placed the communicator on the table. "You can get out of here," he said to Sobrie. "Go to that space city I told you about. They'll receive you; they're very hospitable."

"Like a rat leaving a sinking ship? No, I don't think so. You should go, naturally, Rond. You've no cause to be here in the first place."

"No, I'm staying behind," Heshke said with a sigh. "Not out of any sense of heroism, but because this insane world has given me too much of a spin as it is. Things have been much too hectic for me lately; I was growing more and more tired by the day. This reservation's the only place I've been able to rest, and I like it here."

"Rond is right," Herrick rumbled, "if you have a way of escape you should take it, Sobrie. Not necessarily for your sake, but for Layella's. It would be false heroism to sacrifice her, too, when she's entirely innocent."

Yes, Layella . . . Sobrie pondered. "Couldn't we take some Amhraks off, too?" he suggested shyly. "A few . . . breeding pairs?"

Herrick shook his head, smiling with bittersweet amusement. "Lonely survivors of a vanished race? No one would be found to fill the role. We've long been accustomed to the idea of species death."

"I'll write out a report," Heshke said, "and you can be an envoy to Retort City for Su-Mueng and myself. They ought to be told what Limnich's answer is, anyway."

"I wish you'd come too."

"No, I'm finished with gadding about through space and time. Having to die doesn't worry me; I'm just going to relax and enjoy being alive until the Titans get here."

The vast cavern complex echoed and thundered to the clatter and roar of machinery. Limnich, looking on the scene from the manager's gallery, nodded with satisfaction. So far his inspection tour of the thirteen main installations involved in Operation Century had proved the efficiency of his administration.

His eye swept over the progress reports, abstracting with skill the salient figures. "I see that, starting from baseline, you're twelve per cent ahead of schedule," he commented.

The manager, a rough-looking individual with a hard, lumpy face, was standing stiffly by his side. "That's right, Planetary Leader," he said, pride edging into his voice.

"I'll expect the same rate of progress, namely a twelve per cent increase over projected output – plus your current output – during the next identical period."

"That represents an exponential increase in production, Leader. But if the materials and components arrive as ordered—"

"They will," Limnich told him curtly. He'd found that demanding the near-impossible frequently produced miracles.

Followed by his entourage, he went with the manager the length of the gallery and passed through a tunnel to an adjoining series of caverns: one of the training grounds of the Legions of Kronos. They walked past row after row of sleek time-travelling war machines, each projecting from its launcher as if eager to depart for the future.

From ahead came hoarse shouts and stamping of feet as men were put through the drill designed by psychologists to bring the nervous system to a peak of alertness. Titan-Colonel Brask met Limnich at the entrance to the drill cavern, saluted, and then turned to bellow commands, forming the squads into open-order ranks and standing them to attention. Limnich took his time over the inspection, pausing at nearly every man to look him over, glancing at the special gadgets of the time-combat kits they wore. Meanwhile, from yet another cavern came a massive fuzzy roaring noise: the sound of scores of time travellers warming up.

Finally he pronounced himself satisfied. Brask escorted him to the third cavern where the crews stood by their machines in readiness for the demonstration. At a signal from Brask they filed aboard. Moments later the fuzzy racket intensified and the time travellers all vanished together, fading away to go hurtling in formation through non-time.

"Impressive," said Limnich. "Very impressive."

"It will be even more impressive when they arrive in enemy time loaded to capacity with hydrogen bombs," Brask said with incisive satisfaction.

Brask took the Planetary Leader to his office to discuss various details. While they were there the vidcom rang with a message for Limnich.

The yellow face of the dev Chink, Hueh Su-Mueng, came up on the screen. Only a faint habitual expression of distaste came to Brask's features, and none at all to Limnich's.

"It appears that your ploy has worked, leader," Su-Mueng said. "My instruments tell me Retort City's ship sent down a lighter to the Amhrak reservation, and now has left orbit."

"So soon?" mused Limnich. "But my tip-off can't even have reached Heshke yet. There must be other information pipelines at work—either that or he couldn't stomach life on the reservation!" He smiled unpleasantly.

"I presume that nothing further need delay the expedition?"

"No, I'll issue the requisite orders." The remaining work to be done should only take a week or two, he thought. The drive-units had already been constructed to the Chink's design, and now could be ferried into space to be fitted to the interplanetary spaceships that had been prepared to take them. The men, the weapons, the organisation, were all ready.

It should be a grand adventure, Limnich told himself. He almost wished he could go along.

Herrick had brought in a tape that had appeared on the reconstituted network somehow.

"It shows the closing down of the Bugel reservation," he said to Heshke, a little apologetically. "You needn't watch it if you'd rather not."

"Please go ahead," Heshke told him, though with a tightening in his stomach.

Herrick put the tape on the playback. "This didn't come through the usual channels," he said. "In fact it looks as if it might be a plant."

"A plant?"

"Yes. The Titans might have wanted us to see it."

The tape came to life, feeding the screen a long, roughly edited succession of sequences from the cameras of the official recordists, without any proper order or commentary. After a few minutes Heshke found himself wanting to close his eyes.

The landscape was not unlike the one outside his door: dusty and bare. As the Titan units advanced into it their half-tracks sent up clouds of dust which drifted in from the horizon.

The Bugels were a copper-skinned, pigmy-like people of a comparatively low cultural standing – little more than savages, in fact. Never very numerous, their reservation was a small one. They ran hither and thither before the implacable Titan vehicles, facing their end without dignity but with much excitement and terror.

The Titans herded the Bugels into compounds. They were given injections or else shot, and buried in lime pits.

Heshke imagined the same happening here – the clouds of dust as the exterminators rolled forward (during the wars, when operating behind the lines in dev-populated territory, they'd been known as SMD's – Special Measure Detachments), the compounds, the clerks checking off names against endless lists (though with the Bugels those lists covered only the noble families), the medics giving the injections and the doctors signing death certificates.

From the looks on their faces, the Titans plainly didn't relish their work. They regarded it as unpleasant, distressing – but necessary. It would have been worse if they'd been killing people; but these were only verminous animals.

Why on Earth had the Titans sent the tape into the Amhrak reservation, Heshke wondered? – if in fact they had, as Herrick suspected. To taunt? To strike fear? Perhaps it was an act of nastiness on the part of some hate-filled official.

Herrick was watching the tape placidly, smoking a tobacco roll, as if he were thinking of something else.

13.

Shiu Kung-Chien and his able assistant Leard Ascar had nearly finished setting up the all-sense transmitter when the vidphone at the other end of the observatory tinkled. A cybernetic servitor rolled forward with the screen, on which the face of Prime Minister Hwen Wu looked out.

"Forgive the intrusion," Hwen Wu apologised, "but a matter of greatest urgency has arisen. Evidently our posting that young man Hueh Su-Mueng to Earth, so as to end his 'awkward presence' here, so to speak, has misfired. He has returned with an invasion fleet."

"I take it you refer to those lumpish vessels which have been hovering outside my observatory window for the past hour," Shiu replied with a trace of exasperation. "I had thought they were part of your own improvident plans. Fortunately they appear to rely on reaction motors for close manoeuvring and are no longer jamming our instruments."

"They're entirely the work of Hueh Shao's son and his new friends," Hwen Wu assured him. "That family seems capable of endless mischief. The invaders have discharged four ship-loads of men through the dock, which they now control, and are rapidly discharging the rest. Haven't you heard the rumpus? They're proving quite destructive."

"Yes, I've been aware of an undignified amount of noise and have several times sent out requests for it to be diminished," Shiu said acidly. "Why are you calling me about it?"

"Well, you're a cabinet minister," Hwen Wu pointed out. "I feel we should meet to dicuss the situation. Hueh Su-Mueng has sent a message demanding our unconditional surrender."

The Prime Minister's words were punctuated by a low, distant roar: the sound of an explosion.

"Very well," Shiu consented resignedly. "I'll come at once."

He turned to Ascar as the servitor rolled away with the vidphone. "This really is tiresome," he complained. "Are your countrymen accustomed to behaving like this?"

"I'm afraid so," Ascar said laconically.

"Barbarians!" muttered Shiu.

"May I continue in your absence?" Ascar asked politely.

"Yes, of course . . . you understand everything?"

"Yes, thanks to an unexampled teacher."

Shiu Kung-Chien departed. Ascar, impatient to get on with it, continued checking the work of the servitors, carefully scanning the streams of calligraphic ideograms that came up on the monitor.

It was damned good to get away from desk-work. He'd been hungering for action for some time.

Titan-Major Brourne stood in a large concourse, a sort of intricate plaza, watching the flood of men, materials and weapons that came surging in a disciplined operation through the docking ports. The flowers and shrubs, the miniature trees and tinted screens, had all been trampled down and cast aside to make way for the traffic, which was heading deeper into the space city. The immediate area was solidly secured, ringed by heavy machine guns and even light cannon, and hour by hour came reports of whole districts taken without any show of resistance.

At this rate the whole city would be in his hands in a day.

Already he'd made an excursion into the occupied areas and everything he saw confirmed his instincts. It was exactly as he would have expected: decadence, nothing but decadence. Decadent art, decadent science, decadent customs. The Chinks were effete, ultra-sophisticated, wallowing in sensual pleasure – the whole city was simply an orgy of effeminate prettiness. And the people didn't seem to know how to react to the invasion. They had none of the rude, healthy vigour that made True Man great.

Brourne strode to a small building near the ports where he had set up his field HQ. Hueh Su-Mueng sat looking over a complicated map he'd prepared of the city. As the reports came in he was marking more and more of it in blue, his code for "taken".

The plan of operations was largely his brainchild. His idea was to have the whole city under control before the masters of the Leisure Retort could gather their wits sufficiently to take any

141

effective action. He was striking down toward the bottleneck joining the two retorts, so as to cut off any retreat in that direction or any orders for weapons that might be given to the workers. Once the Leisure Retort had been seized he'd been promised that he himself could take a small force of Titans into the Production Retort. He hoped for a good response from its inhabitants to his news.

"All in order?" Brourne rapped.

Su-Mueng nodded, looking up at the stubby, barrel-like man. "We're keeping to our timetable remarkably well."

"Too well," Brourne rumbled sulkily. "I like the opposition to put up a bit of a fight."

Su-Mueng ignored the remark and continued studying the map, wondering where Hwen Wu and the rest of the cabinet were.

A Titan sergeant appeared at the door and saluted smartly. "We've found a white man, sir."

Brourne turned with interest, but the man who stood there flanked by two troopers was unknown to him. He was a tall, slim man, his eyes steady, wearing garments of an unfamiliar cut – basically Earth style, but probably tailored here in the space city, Brourne imagined.

"Who are you?" he barked.

The other paused before answering in a low tone. "My name is Citizen Sobrie Oblomot."

The Titan-Major glared at him, then decided on a less threatening posture. "Well, it's certainly a change to find a white man in a place like this," he said briskly. "How did you come to be here?"

"A Chink ship brought me," Oblomot told him. "From the Amhrak reservation."

"Amhrak? Are you an Amhrak?" Brourne was startled, almost indignant. "Frankly I wouldn't have known it—"

"No, I'm not Amhrak. I was banished there for . . . political reasons."

"Oh, I see." Brourne grimaced. "As a matter of fact, my men were expecting to find Rond Heshke, the archaeologist, when they brought you in. Presumably he was on the ship too?"

"No . . ." Oblomot said slowly. "Rond stayed behind."

Brourne looked disappointed.

Dismally Sobrie's eyes took in the scene in Brourne's HQ. It depressed him, having thought he'd escaped the Titans for good,

142

to see them come pouring into Retort City as well. For a moment he'd had the crazy idea that they were taking over the universe.

His first thought had been for Layella. Even in Retort City costume she stood out a mile. But a group of women had taken care of her and hidden her somewhere. With luck the Titans wouldn't notice her for some time.

For some reason he hadn't tried to flee himself. Probably, he rationalised, he'd become infected with Rond Heshke's style of defeatism.

The young officer at the table turned around and spoke to the Titan-Major. It was, Sobrie realised with a start, Hueh Su-Mueng – wearing Titan uniform! The spectacle of a full-blooded Chink dressed out as a Titan-Lieutenant made Sobrie burst into laughter.

Brourne silenced him with a scowl and lumbered over to glance at the map. His troops had reached the centre of the city – of this half of the city, at any rate. Even if its rulers tried to organise some sort of defence it would do them no good now.

"Excellent, excellent," he murmured. "Well, there it is, then. The job's practically done."

Su-Mueng rose to his feet and spoke respectfully. "Now that matters have reached this stage, Major, may I request that I lead a force into the Lower Retort, to assess the situation there?"

The Titan laughed brutally. "Sit tight, Chink, you're not going anywhere."

Alarm showed on Su-Mueng's yellow features. "I don't understand, Major. Planetary Leader Limnich made a firm promise—"

"We don't do deals with devs," Brourne sneered. "Sometimes they come in useful, like animals come in useful. You've done your job, and thanks very much." He jerked his head to two huge guards at the back of the room, who promptly strode forward and stamped to attention on either side of Su-Mueng.

The boy's a simpleton, Sobrie thought. He really didn't know what sort of people he was mixing with. He probably doesn't understand, even now, what racism means.

And Su-Mueng did, indeed, look bewildered, like a child who's been cheated.

"This – this is outright treachery!" he spluttered breathlessly, swaying as though about to faint. "When Limnich hears—"

"Limnich, Limnich!" Brourne jeered. He laughed again, loudly. "After you left, Limnich had his office fumigated!"

143

"You need me to get cooperation in the Lower Retort —"

"The Lower Retort will get the same treatment this one is getting – and soon." He would have moved into the Production Retort first, in fact, except that there was no dock there for the spaceships. Still, Brourne didn't anticipate any trouble. The masters are gutless, he thought. The slaves must be even worse.

"If you have any further role to play, it will be as an interpreter," he told Su-Mueng. "We'll probably need a few of those."

He gestured to the guards. "Take him in custody. This fellow Oblomot, too. I'll decide what to do with him later."

Su-Mueng stood blankly for a moment. Then he did an astonishing thing. He took one step to the rear and both hands went smoothly up to both men's necks. The troopers jerked momentarily, then fell back, unconscious.

The lithe youth bounded forward to meet the party escorting Sobrie. His hands seemed scarcely to touch them, merely weaving in and out in a graceful arabesque. But the soldiers were caught up in that arabesque, tumbling in a flurry of limbs until they finished up dazed on the other side of the room.

The people of the Upper Retort practised the arts and all mental pleasures; those of the Lower Retort practised sport. Su-Mueng was using *Hoka*, the culmination of thousands of years' development of unarmed combat. Compared with the enthusiasts in the Production Retort Su-Mueng was but a beginner, but he could stun – or, though that was forbidden, kill – with but a light touch upon a nerve, and in his hands an untrained man's body was but an assemblage of self-destructive levers.

Brourne's gun was in his hand. Su-Mueng too drew his own Corgel automatic in one easy movement – the Titans, treating his honorary rank as one huge joke, had delighted in fitting him out with all accoutrements, including an "honorary certificate of racial purity" – and bent forward in a supple stance, bringing his gun hand forward to shoot the Major carefully in the arm. Brourne swung away, cursing with pain.

Su-Mueng put a hand between Sobrie's shoulder blades and propelled him through the door. Sobrie, surrendering his will, ran with him across the plaza toward the stream of guns and vehicles that bounced across the occasionally uneven flooring.

Glancing behind him, Sobrie saw Brourne struggle to the door, leaning against the jamb. Su-Mueng threw up his hand imperiously, bringing to a halt a light truck.

The driver glanced curiously at him, but he already knew about this strange dev officer; it didn't seem odd to him that he should be hitching a ride, while Sobrie's presence went unremarked. Su-Mueng urged his companion into the covered rear, joined him, and banged on the driving cab for the Titan to continue.

The truck was half-filled with crated ammunition. They settled down tensely as the vehicle jolted forward. "When we're out of the area we'll slip out and make our own way," Su-Mueng said, speaking low.

Sobrie nodded. They rode for some minutes with no apparent sign of danger, and now that he had time free from action Su-Mueng let his dismay and resentment flood like a tide of sickness through his bloodstream.

"Anyone could have told you," Sobrie admonished, noticing his distress. "It was a pretty silly thing to do, tying yourself in with the Titans."

"I thought I would give my father's death some meaning," Su-Mueng answered. "Never again would a man die for loving his son. . . ."

He trailed off, realising that Sobrie didn't know what he was talking about. His face creased in a pondering frown. "Perhaps the Titans will go away again when they have what they want."

"Not likely. They'll probably try to fly this city to the solar system and orbit it somewhere. It gives them a ready-made industrial system, complete with millions of trained slaves, and they'll make all the use they can of it, for a long time to come. Even if they decide to abandon it, they wouldn't leave anybody alive," he ended. "To their way of thinking you people are a blot on nature. I'm amazed you couldn't see it."

"I knew they hold to some sort of biological creed, of course," Su-Mueng admitted grudgingly, "but I hadn't supposed it would make any difference. Ours was a practical arrangement purely, to our mutual advantage – as I thought. There was no conflict of interests."

"Ah well, I suppose it would have gone the same way whatever race you belonged to," Sobrie sighed. "The Titans always seek only their own advantage – never anyone else's."

Su-Mueng was silent for a while. "It's all yet another indictment of Retort City's social methods," he said then, grinding the words out. "I was brought up in a closed system, unable to adapt myself to the mores of another world."

145

"Your remarks, nevertheless, are acute," said Sobrie with a wry smile. "All you need is a chance. But where exactly are we supposed to be going?"

"Having brought disaster to my city, the least I can do is to try to rectify the situation. Perhaps something can be salvaged from all this yet."

"I'd like to know how you're going to do that, young man."

Su-Mueng brooded, and after a while peered out of the back of the truck.

"Here," he commanded.

They dropped lightly from the truck, stumbled, and ran for the shelter of a grove of willow trees. The convoy passed by without pause.

Behind the grove was a colonnade flanked by walls slatted and louvered in rosewood. They set off down this and then Su-Mueng, hesitating frequently, led Sobrie on a long, circuitous tour of the Leisure Retort.

Sobrie, who wasn't yet very familiar with the retort, saw much that was new to him. The beauty of the place was offset, to some extent, by the ubiquitous black-and-gold Titan uniforms. Amazingly, no general order for their arrest seemed to have gone out and Su-Mueng was several times saluted smartly by patrolling troops.

An unreal air pervaded the city. The inhabitants, contrasting sharply in appearance with their newly arrived conquerors, displayed no apparent alarm. There was much laughing and joking as the sweating Titans set up their emplacements. If Sobrie hadn't already sampled the mental sophistication of these people, he would have thought them to be simple children who didn't know what was happening.

At last they entered what Sobrie took to be a nursery. Cribs lined the walls of a sunny room, nearly every crib bearing a baby. All, Sobrie guessed, were newborn.

He couldn't imagine why Su-Mueng should have brought him to a maternity ward. A young woman came forward, inclining her head while Su-Mueng spoke to her rapidly in a low voice. She frowned, looked doubtful and incredulous by turns, and then the two of them went off somewhere together.

Sobrie was beginning to feel uneasy by the time Su-Mueng returned. "They've agreed to it," the young man said. "It's kind of hard to get these people to admit there's an emergency afoot.

I thought I was going to have to use force."

"They've agreed to what?" Sobrie asked, following the other. They passed along a corridor, smelling pleasantly of perfumes, and came to a chamber that evidently served some function not clear to Sobrie. There were cradles, set on rails that vanished into the wall. A barely perceptible hum filled the air.

"We're going down into the Production Retort," Su-Mueng informed him. Men entered the chamber, removed the cradles and replaced them with a platform on which were mounted a number of padded chairs.

One of them grinned cheerfully at Su-Mueng. "A long time since this was last used," he said.

At his direction Sobrie seated himself in one of the chairs beside Su-Mueng. The wall facing them rolled away, revealing a tunnel that dwindled into the distance.

Su-Mueng's expression was matter-of-fact. The platform moved into the tunnel, which was unlit and soon pitch-black. They travelled smoothly, without noticeable acceleration – without, indeed, any noticeable breeze – but Sobrie became aware of an unusual feeling, as if he were being lifted and compressed at the same time, and the faint hum intensified. After perhaps two minutes a light showed ahead, brightening until they emerged into a chamber much like the one they'd left.

Su-Mueng leaped up from his chair, shouting excitedly at the receptionists, young women who seemed astonished at their arrival. Sobrie followed him as he dashed into an adjoining chamber. From nearby he heard the crying of very young babies.

There were no babies, however, in the room in which Sobrie found himself. There was a bank of instruments and controls arranged in a workmanlike way around a bucket seat and desk. In that seat was a controller – but dressed in a simple blue garb rather than the sumptuous finery Sobrie had come to expect in the Leisure Retort.

Energetically Su-Mueng pushed the controller aside and applied himself with great concentration to the controls. The displaced controller gawped from the floor, too staggered to rise.

The ever-present hum that lay just within the bounds of audibility died into silence. With satisfaction Su-Mueng drew his automatic and fired several times into the main switch, sealing the settings temporarily at least.

The two retorts were now totally separated in time: no time-

147

gradient connected them. If the Titans were to come along the tunnel Sobrie and Su-Mueng had just travelled, or to enter by any other route, they would only arrive into its unpeopled future.

Su-Mueng turned to the controller he'd just treated so barbarically. "Come with me," he said. "It's imperative that I speak with the retort managers!"

"We've captured the ruling clique, sir."

"All right, let me see them."

Brourne stared at the impassive, droopy-moustached, silky-bearded, satined and silked old men who came up on the screen. "How do you know this is the ruling clique?" he demanded.

The youthful, enthusiastic Captain came back into view. "They admit it, sir. We've found a kind of computer that knows a few Earth phrases."

"Oh? How many?"

"Not enough for a useful interrogation, I'm afraid."

"I see. Well, lock them up until later."

"Yes, sir." The Captain snapped off a salute and went off the line.

Brourne turned away, gingerly massaging his injured arm, which lay in a sling. What was the point of capturing anybody when he couldn't talk to them? He cursed again for having let Hueh Su-Mueng get away. At the time he'd thought nothing of it, hadn't even ordered any pursuit or search. Why bother? The Chink's first move had doubtless been to divest himself of his uniform, whereupon he might as well have been invisible. It was practically impossible to tell these Chinks apart.

There was another possibility, Brourne reminded himself. Leard Ascar was still in the city somewhere and sooner or later his men would find him. By all accounts Ascar was an intractable, un-balanced personality – in his preflight briefing Brourne had been advised that he was "unreliable" – but presumably he knew the language, as Heshke had. He would have to do.

The vidcom burred again. Brourne returned to it.

"HQ. Major Brourne."

A serious-faced tech officer gazed out at him. "The sortie to the lower retort has sent back a report, sir."

"Yes?"

"They say it's deserted. Crammed full of factories and work-shops – but there's not a single human being there."

"Deserted? You're sure they're not hiding out somewhere?"

"That's not how things look, and no one's been found yet."

"So maybe that cur of a Chink was lying," Brourne responded. "The whole place could be automated – no workers at all."

"Perhaps – but again, that's not how it looks. Right now there's not a wheel turning. And there are signs of decay, as though the whole complex had been abandoned about fifty years ago."

Brourne became thoughtful. "That doesn't figure," he rumbled. "It doesn't figure at all. Wasn't there supposed to be something about the two halves of the city not matching in time?"

"Our men simply went through a tunnel about a third of a mile long," the tech said. "But there are other ways in. There's a marshalling yard where the produce of the factories comes through. I'll investigate further."

"Do that. And keep me informed."

Right now, he thought, is where Leard Ascar would really come in handy.

Ascar was trembling with excitement.

During the past few weeks Shiu Kung-Chien had told him a great deal about the Oblique Entity that had once nearly annihilated Retort City – as much, indeed, as the elder scientist himself knew. Ascar had begged that he, too, be allowed to visit this strange intelligence via the all-sense sender, but Shiu had prevailed upon him to delay the experience. The all-sense transmissions, crude at the moment, needed refining.

And so Ascar had worked patiently under the old man's direction, studying and thinking deeply. The Oblique Entity, Shiu had intimated, had powers beyond the merely human. It wasn't a biological intelligence; it wasn't associated with any planet or celestial body; its nature, though it had a material structure, wasn't readily intelligible to human beings.

During the last phase of their work to improve the transceiver the Titans had arrived and invaded the ISS. Shiu, imperturbable as ever (Ascar was impressed by the way any event, no matter how grave, failed to shake the placidity of the people here; they were, Shiu had told him once, dilettantes at everything, even living), had left Ascar to carry on, which he did while the noises of destruction as the Titans pulled down sections of the city to facilitate their easy movement grew nearer and nearer.

For the past half hour the sounds of conquest had died down.

Presumably the Leisure Retort was now in the Titans' grip, which meant that they'd soon be battering down his door. He was anxious to have made his trip before they did that, because they would very likely deprive him of any further opportunity and he was impelled by more than mere intellectual curiosity. Some time ago he'd asked Shiu Kung-Chien how the Oblique Entity's own knowledge of the physical universe compared with their own.

Shiu Kung-Chien had hesitated. Compared with men, he'd said, the Oblique Entity had knowledge that was like that "of one of your ancient gods".

Ascar had some very definite questions to put to this entity.

And so Ascar completed the countdown. Shiu had already completed a trial run with the new equipment; all Ascar had to do now was to make the final checks.

The flickering ideograms froze at last; the apparatus was poised in readiness. He rubbed his eyes. Although he'd been trained in a matter of minutes to read the specialised calligraphy Shiu used, he still found the ideograms hard to focus on at speed.

He glanced over the big, gleaming, block-like transformers of time energy that were dumped unceremoniously in the middle of the observatory, humming fuzzily. They had, he supposed, taken a couple of years to manufacture, yet they'd been delivered to Shiu within an hour of his submitting the designs. Such was the nature of the resources he could draw on: resources he used so carelessly, and in so cavalier a fashion, that Ascar was constantly amazed. He'd order new equipment with absolutely no thought for the labour time involved, drawing up version after version of some difficult design and demanding an operating model of each so as to try out his various (and sometimes offhand) ideas. His storeroom was jammed with machinery, much of it never used, and many items that arrived were sent back to be scrapped after a few desultory experiments.

The Oblique Entity was already reciprocating on their contact stream, expressing its willingness for the exchange. The cybernetic servitor moved into position to operate the equipment. His heart thumping, Ascar stepped into the transparent sphere. The hatch closed behind him as he sat down in the central chair, and then he was in darkness.

The transceiver seized his senses and snatched them out of intelligible time, hurling them in a direction no compass could ever find.

At first there was only silence, and continued darkness. Then out of that darkness a voice said suddenly: "I am here. You have arrived. What do you want?"

The voice, though loud, was smooth and confidential. It seemed to be spoken close to his ear – or rather, to both his ears. Behind the voice was a silence, but behind that silence Ascar fancied he could hear a whispering whistle, like the susurration that sometimes accompanied radio transmissions.

"I want to see you," Ascar said into the darkness.

"How do you wish to see me?"

Ascar didn't understand the question for a moment; then he answered: "I want to see you as you are."

"Very well. Here is our physical reality."

The change was brutally abrupt. Ascar suddenly found himself amid an uproar in a long gallery. He was kneeling, for the height of the gallery was only about four feet and gave approximately the same room on either side, though it stretched away ahead of him seemingly into infinity. Furthermore it was only one of a multitude of such structures arranged around him, and which he glimpsed through the iron frameworks separating them. And those frameworks contained —

He inspected the complex closely. As near as he could judge, the objects would best be described as machines. The galleries were, in fact, avenues for the siting of a continuous machine process which clattered, rotated and shuffled through indefinably intricate operations. Ascar was in the midst of a roaring, close-packed factory of vast extent, like some industrialised hell.

"Did you construct this?" he asked into thin air.

"No," came the immediate answer, easily audible despite the deafening racket. "This *is* us – a small part of me. All this came into existence spontaneously, as a result of the process of time. I/We is not biological."

Ascar felt himself moving forward. The floor offered no perceptible resistance to his knees, but a hot wind played against his face. The endless galleries swept past blurrily as he gathered speed and went darting into a claustrophobic infinity.

Then, without warning, he came to a stop. The machine complex was behind him in the form of a towering serried wall; its array, he recognised, was reminiscent of the array of atoms in a metal.

He faced now a huge gulf from whose depths came tumultuous

boiling, a giving forth of steam clouds and acid vapours which seared his skin. Its size was impossible to judge. Ascar moved along the edge of this infernal pit until he came to another of its boundaries: a second wall of solid-packed quasi-machinery. But this time there were no narrow galleries through the honeycomb; the whole mass was impenetrable, none of its interstices being large enough to admit his body.

He glanced overhead, attracted by a regular, gigantic noise. Slanting obliquely over the space above him was something like a moving belt, or a high-speed printing press. It roared on its way at a colossal speed, for all that it must have been a hundred miles long.

"Perhaps you would prefer to meet me in different surroundings," the Oblique Entity said. Everything vanished, and was replaced.

Ascar was sitting in a moderately sized room. The walls were of pale blue decorated with a white cornice. The light, coming from an unseen source, was very radiant, reminding him of sunlight. Before Ascar stood a table of polished walnut.

A door opened. In walked a young woman who sat down opposite him. Her skin was silver-blue. A slight smile was on her lips. Her eyes were bright blue, also, but they looked beyond, Ascar, as if they weren't functional.

"Good day," she said in a pleasant, full voice. "Is this more agreeable?"

Ascar took a moment to recover himself. "But this isn't you as you really are, is it?" he said then.

"No, that is true."

Ascar was vaguely disappointed. "Then it's just an illusion you're putting through the all-sense receiver. I didn't come all this way looking for illusions."

"Incorrect: it is no illusion. I have constructed the environment as a physical reality, into which I then projected your senses. Even the woman is a real living woman."

Now Ascar was startled. "You can do that – in a moment?"

A pause. "Not in a moment, exactly. To produce the woman took a hundred years. Duration is of no consequence when time can be turned in a circle."

So that was it, Ascar thought. It was the Production Retort all over again, but on an even larger scale. Here, the beginning and the end of a lengthy process could be bent around to occupy successive moments. He mulled over another point.

"Sometimes you call yourself *I*, and sometimes *we*," he observed. "What are you, a single intelligence or a community?"

"I am neither individual nor plural," the Oblique Entity replied. "Neither *I* nor *we* is adequate to describe my nature."

"Then just what *are* you?"

The girl inclined her head, her eyes seeking a point beyond the wall, and a slight, quizzical frown crossed her features.

"Perhaps these surroundings, even, are disconcerting?" she suggested. "Let us try again."

She rose, and pointed to a second door that opened itself behind Ascar. "Please continue on down the corridor," she invited. "Another room has been prepared."

After a last doubtful glance at the girl Ascar obeyed. At first the corridor was featureless, grey and doorless, stretching away to a bend, or dead-end, about two hundred yards ahead. But as he proceeded a peculiar illusion began to occur. Out of the corner of his eye he glimpsed arcaded openings beyond which fish-like shapes flitted among green stalks and through wavering groves. Yet when he turned his head to look directly at this phenomenon his eye met only a blank wall.

He began to get the odd feeling that the elusive fish-shapes flitted, not externally, but through the recesses of his own mind. After a few tens of yards, however, the illusion ceased. But at the same time the character of the corridor began to change subtly, to become less featureless and more familiar. Suddenly Ascar stopped. He had come to a door: a door with the number 22 stencilled on it.

He looked around him. Just ahead was a T-junction, where arrowed notices pointed out departments in either direction. He looked again at the door with the number 22, recognising scratch marks and pimples in the paint.

This place was a corridor in the Sarn Establishment! Or a perfect replica thereof.

With thumping heart he opened the door. Within was a cosy, cabin-like room with a bunk, chairs, and a table strewn with abstracts and reports together with a large scratch-pad. The wall to his left was a bookcase holding a small library of specialised volumes.

It was his own room and refuge that he'd inhabited for five years.

Slowly he closed the door and sat down in his favourite chair, realising as he did so that the Oblique Entity must have extracted all these details from his own memory.

Above the door was a small speaker that had been used in the Sarn Establishment for paging. The Oblique Entity spoke now through this grill.

"To answer your question," it said in its former male voice, "the type of consciousness I possess is neither an individual consciousness, nor is it a group consciousness or a community of individuals. In your language I could come closer to the facts simply by referring to ourselves as *here*, rather than to *I* or *we*. Henceforth, then I will give ourselves the personal pronoun *here*."

Ascar pondered that, nodding. The Entity's ploy, he decided, was working. He *did* feel more relaxed to be sitting here in his own room. It would have been easy to forget altogether that this was not, in fact, the Sarn Establishment.

"Since you can evidently read my mind, you already know what I mean to ask you," he said. "Tell me, how much do you know of Earth?"

"Here know all about Earth," the Oblique Entity replied.

"You mean you've read all about it in my mind?"

"No. Here knew about Earth already. By direct observation."

"Then you know what's about to happen there?"

"Yes."

"Then," said Ascar, giving his words emphasis and deliberation, "is there any way – any way at all – that the stream of time can be turned aside or stopped? Any way that collision can be avoided?"

The Oblique Entity didn't answer immediately. Instead, a rich humming note issued from the speaker. All at once everything exploded around Ascar. He was floating in an inchoate void. Around him swam coloured shapes of every description, drifting in and out of his vision like sparks.

His body seemed to become elongated, like a streamer of smoke in a breeze; he was being stretched out to infinity. This process seemed to go on for a long, long time; and then, just as suddenly, he was back in his favourite chair in his comfortable room.

"There is nothing *you* can do," the Oblique Entity said.

When Brourne's troops finally broke into the space-time observatory they found Leard Ascar still sitting in the transparent

154

sphere of the all-sense transceiver.

After a matter of minutes they contrived to open the hatch. Ascar appeared not to see them. He sat muttering unintelligibly to himself, offering no resistance when they grabbed him by the arms and hauled him out.

"This must be Ascar," the sergeant said. "If you ask me these Chink gadgets have driven him out of his mind!"

"Maybe he's fallen foul of a Chink puzzle," a trooper offered helpfully.

"Eh? What?" Ascar began to come round, peering at the trooper with narrowed eyes.

"Let's get him away from here," the sergeant ordered. "Major Brourne wants to see him right away."

They steered Ascar out of the observatory. And then an unexpected sound caused them all at once to come to a stop and gaze at one another wonderingly. For some hours the city had been quiet, but now, from the distance, came the sudden, continuous eruption of heavy gunfire.

Heshke accepted a tobacco roll, inhaling the fragrant smoke with a sense of special pleasure.

It was, in the fullest sense, a farewell party. They all knew that the Titans would come rolling into the reservation tomorrow, or at the latest the day after. Herrick had called together a few of his friends, as he put it, to "celebrate the end of the species".

The atmosphere was relaxed and convivial. Heshke couldn't help but admire the calm way the Amhraks were accepting the inevitable. Perhaps, he thought, it was the inevitability that lent such dignity. If there had been any hope at all, that might have led to panic.

Much of the conversation was in Amhrak, at which Heshke was not as yet very skilled. However, out of politeness, enough Verolian – the main language of white men that was used all over the Earth now – was spoken so that he felt by no means left out.

A lanky Amhrak girl chatted to him, sipping a glass of wine synthesised by a newly perfected process. "You must find our village rather dull after Pradna," she said, smiling.

"I wasn't actually in Pradna," he told her. "I spent most of my time in the field, working on alien ruins. Pradna is a pretty ghastly place anyway, to tell you the truth. I like it much better here . . .

in spite of what's happening."

As he spoke the last words he had the sinking feeling of having committed a *faux pas*. These people could have a taboo about speaking of . . . *that*, he thought timidly. But the girl merely laughed, quite without strain.

"It must be *really* awful in Pradna," she joked, "to prefer *that*."

Herrick had opened the double doors of his workshop and was fiddling with his transmitterless television receiver. To hide his embarrassment Heshke joined him, and for some minutes Herrick phased through the magnetowaves, seeking coherent visuals and gaining more than the usual number.

"Conditions are remarkably conducive tonight," Herrick commented with some surprise. "The nodes are particularly strong. Here comes a good one."

The view, as most of them were, was from the air. It showed the outskirts of a town of moderate size, judging by the layout of the buildings. The angle of the sun revealed the time to be midafternoon.

"Do you recognise it?" Herrick asked him.

Heshke shook his head. It could have been any of a thousand such towns.

Instead of dissipating after a few seconds, which was what normally happened, the picture lingered. Herrick managed to steady it further, until the quality was almost of commercial standard.

"At last I'm getting somewhere," Herrick said sadly. "It seems a pity to – *what's that?*"

The frame of the picture itself remained steady and bright; but certain elements in it were fading. While the two men watched (Heshke was vaguely aware of other eyes peering over his shoulder through the double doors) all the buildings in the picture seemed to melt away, leaving a bare background. Not only that, but a grove of trees also vanished, together with a stretch of grass.

What remained was bare, arid soil.

"Some effect of the system?" Heshke suggested mildly.

"I don't see how," Herrick muttered. "There are television systems that *could* produce this effect – systems employing a memory bank to hold persistent elements in the picture, so that it's built up piece by piece – but I rely on a simple scanning procedure. Look, you can see the places where those buildings had stood. It's just as if the whole town had disappeared into thin air."

156

"Then you must have been picking up two different images superimposed," Heshke said. "One faded out and you're left with the other."

"Yes, that might explain it." Herrick nodded reluctantly. "That must be it. But as to how they came to blend so perfectly – and I thought I'd licked the tuning problem, too."

Heshke wandered out of the room, leaving Herrick still absorbed in his apparatus.

He went onto the verandah and looked out over the desert. The night sky seemed to hold a strange, flickering light, as if lightning was playing somewhere beyond the horizon.

The attempted return to Brourne's HQ was hectic.

They'd gone about half a mile in the squad's armoured runabout – the Titans scorned to use Retort City's own public transport system – when they came upon one of the main arteries that had been cleared to give the city's new masters easy access. The highway was thundering with traffic, all of it heading toward the sound of bombs and gunfire that came from the city's bottleneck end.

"Toward the front," muttered the sergeant.

The wild looks on the faces of the Titans who clung to the swaying gun carriages told them that the situation had more than a measure of desperation. No natives were in sight: presumably they were all huddling somewhere, terrified of Titan savagery when the going got tough. A Titan soldier, for example, would shoot anyone who happened to be standing in his way when a sense of urgency overtook him.

"What in the Mother's name is going on, sarge?" one of the troopers asked.

"Must be something big." He ruminated. "Maybe the Chinks were holding onto their defences." He nudged the driver. "Our job is to get this man to HQ. Get across the highway when there's a gap and go by way of the secondary route."

The highway came in from the main supply dump, close to the dock. HQ was in a central part of the city. Eventually they crossed the busy viaduct and continued, past empty tiers, galleries and plazas.

"This place gives me the creeps," someone grumbled. "I'll be glad to get back to Pradna."

Ahead of them was a machine gun post. Troopers yelled at

them, brought them to a halt.

"You can't go up there," a corporal told them, "it's cut off."

"Cut off by *who?*"

"The Chinks have an army," the corporal said stolidly. "Everything's in chaos."

Suddenly the machine gun gave out a short stuttering burst. "Here they come!" yelled the man firing it.

The sergeant reached into the runabout and brought out his burp gun. He could see them, too, now, emerging from the end of a tree-lined avenue. They wore rough, blue uniforms and wide-brimmed dome helmets.

He rapped out orders. The armoured runabout proceeded slowly up the avenue, its occupants firing from its slits. He stayed with the machine gun crew, down on one knee, peering over the barricade and fingering his burp gun.

And then, without any warning, the Chinks were upon them: all around them, as if they'd dropped from the nonexistent sky.

Titan-Major Brourne knew already that he'd committed a tactical error when he moved his HQ from the cramped accommodation at the dockside to his present palatial quarters near the centre of the city.

At the time it had seemed reasonable. The city had been taken. He needed an administrative centre, and the dock just wouldn't do.

But now, up through the bottleneck from the Production Retort which all his scouts had assured him was empty, had come a huge army, well-prepared and well-disciplined. Brourne still only had an inkling of where this army had really come from, but in any case explanations, at this stage, were very low down on his list of priorities.

When it first became clear that the threat was serious he'd given thought to the route back to the dock, to a withdrawal to the ships floating outside the city if necessary. With deep chagrin he learned that the dock was one of the first points to be seized by the enemy. His forces were still trying to retake it.

Elsewhere the story was one of repeated disaster. The invasion force was overwhelming, and none of the measures he'd taken to retain military control seemed effective. The Chinks were able to flit in and out of existence like shadows, by means of some device they possessed, apparently, and so were able to infiltrate

158

all his fixed defences. They carried only light arms and knives, but more often than not fought using an unarmed combat technique that was as deadly as anything he'd come across.

His ire rising, Brourne listened to the distressing tale of section after section of the city falling, of the enemy appearing simultaneously everywhere, that the battle reports told. He slammed down the key that opened the line to all district commanders. For some minutes now they'd been requesting instructions.

"Kill everything that moves!" he roared. "Have you got that? Everything that moves!"

"Haven't I met you somewhere?" Leard Ascar asked, squinting quizzically at the white man wearing the uniform of the Lower Retort invaders.

"Sobrie Oblomot." The other smiled. "We met twice, a few days ago. For you it was a few days ago, that is; for me it was more than a year."

"Oh yes, that's right," Ascar muttered. "You came in on the ship from Earth, in Rond Heshke's place. Forgive me, I've a poor memory for faces." He waved a hand negligently. "So the Titans haven't had it all their own way?"

Sobrie allowed himself a look of quiet triumph. "They don't know what's hit them. You know the secret of the Lower Retort's success, of course -- that it can always take as much time as it needs to work on something, even when results are required in minutes. We only spent a year in organising our onslaught, but we could have taken twenty-five years if need be."

"Yes, I thought there would be something like that," Ascar said. "I'm surprised the Titans let you pull off such a stunt."

"They had no opportunity to stop us. Do you remember a young man by the name of Hueh Su-Mueng? The Titans brought him with them, back from Earth. They'd have done better to leave him behind: he switched off the time tunnel between the two retorts, denying the Titans access to it, in its normative time, at least. I expect they could have found their way into it with the new ships they have, but we were upon them before they fully realised what was going on. In Leisure Retort time, Su-Mueng and myself were back within an hour of leaving -- with a fully-equipped and trained army!"

Ascar grunted. "Somebody on Limnich's staff goofed. Not that it matters." He stretched. He'd been separated from the Titan prisoners and put in more luxurious surroundings reserved, he guessed, for detainees of more exalted rank. Oblomot's visit, however, had been a surprise.

"I remember you now," he said. "You're some kind of revolutionary nut, aren't you? A dev-lover. Yes, that's right."

"Say what you like. I'm not alone: Su-Mueng is a revolutionary too. Things are going to change around here."

"If you're expecting the Production Retort workers to toe some kind of rebellion line, forget it," Ascar told him. "People know how to arrange society in this ISS. It's orderly."

"Well, we'll see. Su-Mueng is an extraordinary person in some ways. It's really impressive the way he was able to get things organised in the Lower Retort. And we've saved Retort City!" Boastfulness crept into Sobrie's voice.

"They respond naturally to being organised down there," Ascar retorted. "It doesn't mean a damn thing." He yawned. He felt tired. "So you've saved Retort City, have you? Well, bend a knee to *me*, friend. You're looking at the man who's saved the planet Earth!"

"You . . . ?" began Sobrie wonderingly, but he was interrupted by a call from outside the apartment.

Hueh Su-Mueng entered. He glanced disdainfully at Ascar, then turned to Sobrie.

"All goes well. The retort is ours, apart from a few pockets of resistance. Also, we've found out where the Earthmen were holding the Leisure Retort cabinet. They should be arriving here soon!"

"Good!" said Ascar vigorously. "Since this little fiasco is finished, I take it my master Shiu Kung-Chien can now return to his observatory and attend matters of greater import. And if you don't mind, I'd like to join him."

"Oh yes, I recognise you," Su-Mueng said. "You're the man who preferred to devote himself to abstract things, rather than try to help his own people. Go on your way, by all means. We have no use for you here." There was a new hardness in the young man, Ascar noted. The past year had changed him.

"Wait!" Sobrie interjected. "What was that you were saying just now – about Earth?"

Ascar put on a stubborn face and folded his arms. "I want to see Shiu Kung-Chien."

"I see what's in your mind," Su-Mueng said after a moment. "You're afraid that I'll execute all the cabinet ministers, includ-

160

ing your beloved master. Don't worry, that's for the people to decide, not me. Perhaps he'll be put to work in a factory, to discover what it's like."

He gave the word to Sobrie, who went out and returned a few minutes later with Shiu. The aged scientist murmured a perfunctory greeting as he entered the room, then spoke to Ascar.

"Was there time to complete the operation?" he asked.

"Just about," said Ascar. "I visited the Oblique Entity, anyway."

"And did you learn anything encouraging?"

"It depends which way you look at it – but yes, you could say I did."

He turned to Sobrie. "You're an Earthman, I suppose, so I'll try to explain. You see, my efforts haven't been quite as devoid of practical motive as might be imagined. Several light-years from here there exists an . . . intelligence, an entity that has been known to Retort City for some time. It's called the Oblique Entity, because it exists obliquely in time. Our object – mine and Shiu's – has been to establish a good enough communication with this entity for an exchange of practical knowledge. Its understanding of the time process is much more profound than ours; consequently I was anxious to find out if it could help us, if there was any way available to science of controlling the onrush of time-systems so as to avert the impending collision on Earth."

"I . . . think I see," Sobrie said in a subdued tone. He felt slightly ashamed of having misjudged Ascar, whom hitherto he'd taken to be little more than a dropout.

Ascar looked at Shiu before continuing. "To my surprise, sir, the Entity already knew about Earth. It makes a hobby, apparently, of watching planets where life exists. I was even more staggered to hear it admit that it has the power, if it chooses, to prevent the cataclysm there. It's able to exert an influence over the direction of time, even upon so massive a system as Earth's and even at so great a distance. Don't ask me how. But it did make it quite clear to me that this power is something human beings will never learn to control."

"But that makes it like a god!" Sobrie exclaimed disbelievingly.

"Yes, like a god," Ascar repeated, his lips curling slightly. That was exactly what he'd said at the time, and the Entity's reply still sounded in his ears: *I am as insignificant as you. The Supreme*

161

does not notice me, just as it does not notice you.

"Is he speaking the truth?" Sobrie asked Shiu anxiously. "Is that really what you've been doing in your observatory?"

Shiu's tone was cold and superior. "That was indeed our project. I'd suspected long ago that the Oblique Entity has powers unknown to us."

"*Deus ex machina,*" Sobrie muttered.

"Yes," said Ascar tonelessly, "a real *deus ex machina.* However, the Oblique Entity insists it's basically a spectator, a non-interventionist. When I asked it to use its powers on our behalf, it refused."

A heavy silence fell on the room, and Su-Mueng stirred.

"My regrets for your planet," he said stiffly. "However, if you'll excuse me, Retort City will continue to exist and I have business to deal with."

"That wasn't the end of the matter, sir," Ascar said quickly to Shiu when the younger man had left the room, "I argued with it further."

His mind fled back to his recent experience, still fresh in his memory. At first his world-weary cynicism had come to the fore. He'd shrugged his shoulders and mentally written Earth off.

But then he'd found that he was unable to give up so easily. Something in him had pushed him on, made him press his case to this being beside which he felt like an ant. He didn't plead, exactly – no, plead wouldn't be the right word – but he'd come close to it.

The Oblique Entity had answered in a throbbing voice. "There is considerable drama in this situation on Earth," it had said. "I am reluctant to interfere with that drama."

For periods during their discourse the room in which Ascar sat had wavered and vanished, and he'd found himself drifting like a dust-mote through vast ratcheting machine-spaces, or through dark emptinesses in which swam flimmering, half-seen shapes. This was not, he decided eventually, an attempt to frighten him or a show of anger on the Entity's part. It was simply that its thought processes occasionally distracted its attention from the job of transmitting sensory data to the receiver in Retort City, and Ascar was left picking up random images. Each time the Entity spoke, however, he was promptly deposited back in his simulated room.

Then, finally, the voice had changed. Ascar had heard the girl's voice again, coming through the speaker with a tinkly laugh.

"Enterprise such as yours deserves a reward," she'd said. "This is what I will do."

And the Entity had shown him, not in words, but in a graphic, simple demonstration that had jolted right into his consciousness. It showed him time being split up into rivulets and streaming in all directions to bring deserts to life. And it showed him the main torrent from which those rivulets were taken, rushing headlong to where it would meet with an equal power and be convulsed into a horrendous vortex that would destroy it.

When Ascar explained this to Shiu the old man nodded, reflecting at length.

"Ingenious," he said. "And logical. The Oblique Entity clearly has a sense of justice."

"I don't understand," Sobrie Oblomot complained. "I don't understand any of it."

Shiu glanced at him and then wrapped his arms in his sleeves. "It would be difficult for a layman," he admitted in his slow, musing voice. "Attend to the following description. Time moves forward, always in one direction. But there is more than just one direction in the real universe. Six dimensions can be defined, not just the three that the Absolute Present produces. So outside the stream of time that travels from the past into the future, there is yet more non-time, like a landscape through which the river of time flows. What this means in practical terms is that there are alternate Earths existing in the fifth dimension, side by side with the Earth you know. These Earths are uninhabited: they have no life, and no time. The river of time could be turned aside so as to flow into one of these alternate Earths, instead of directly onward. There would be no collision; an ideal solution to your problem."

"And that, I take it, is not to be?" Sobrie asked, wrestling with these abstract ideas.

"Regretfully, no. The Entity is leaving the main stream of Earth's time untouched. It agrees only to split off rivulets from the main flow, sending each into a different Earth – there are a vast number to choose from, all more or less the same. The people involved in these rivulets will find themselves constituting a small island of life in an otherwise desert planet. But eventually that life will spread to cover the whole globe. In each case a new world will be born." He nodded to himself, an unselfconscious

163

picture of sagacity. "It is, perhaps, a wiser solution than we would have chosen."

"Each surviving dev reservation will be given a world of its own," Ascar explained to Sobrie. "The Oblique Entity is giving every human subspecies its own future, free of interference from any other. A contingent of Titan civilisation, even, is being given its own Earth to rule – an Earth where there will be no alien interventionists, no future-Earth aliens to destroy Titan ambitions. And the same holds for the future-Earth race: they also have various factions and nations, some of which will be saved."

"And for the rest – annihilation?"

"Yes – almost." A gleam, as of a vision, came into Ascar's eyes. "The Armageddon, the great war through time, must take place, as must the collision in time. But even there, there will be survivors. Even now the Titans are drawing up blueprints for protective bunkers, buffered with intense artificial time fields to try to ward off the force of the collision. Some of these bunkers – a few – will probably survive, provided their equipment is rugged enough. So there will be a handful of Titans left alive after it's all over, to try to rebuild something on an Earth that will be unimaginably devastated."

"This splitting up of time – when is it going to happen?"

"It already has happened," Ascar said. "It had happened before the Titans found me in Shiu's observatory."

Sobrie wondered if his friends in the Amhrak reservation had noticed their changed circumstances yet. It was good, he thought to himself, to know that Amhrak civilisation *would* continue.

Titan-Major Brourne flung the array of vidcoms off the table with one sweep of his arm. Nobody was reporting in now.

Brourne was alone in his office; he'd already sent his adjutant outside to help man the barricade. The time had come, he saw, for the last stand.

He strode from the office. As far as he knew his HQ was the only post not yet overrun, and an attack was expected any second.

A long gallery-like concourse stretched ahead of the building he'd chosen for his headquarters. It gave an excellent defensive position: a long avenue, bare of cover, up which an enemy must pass. But that would avail little, he knew, against the tricks of these Chinks.

He'd barely reached the steel barricade set up across this

avenue, and was giving a few words of encouragement to his men, when the attack started.

The Chinks were everywhere simultaneously. Several appeared on his side of the barricade and some of his men set to fighting them furiously at close quarters, while others were firing stolidly down the avenue. Once again Brourne observed the dreadful effects of *Hoka*, but fortunately the Chinks here were outnumbered. Then he directed his eyes down the avenue. There they were: blue-uniformed, broad-helmeted, flitting in and out of existence and advancing down the concourse like shadowy ghosts. He was facing an enemy one could only see half the time.

Suddenly Major Brourne gave a violent, almost joyous roar. He leaped forward to a gun emplacement, pushed the gunner aside, and lifted the heavy machine gun off its tripod. Normally two men were needed to carry it, but Brourne clambered over the barricade, the cartridge belt trailing behind him, and fired a long burst from the hip.

"No use squatting here, men!" he bellowed. "Come on out and get 'em!"

He went lumbering down the concourse, firing intermittently from the big, clumsy weapon, into the crowd of flitting Chinks. This was the way to go, he told himself. To die like a man, fighting to the last breath against a subhuman horde.

He was still firing when a hand touched the back of his neck and he died.

The blue-garbed soldiers thronged the plaza before the balcony where Su-Mueng, Sobrie and Prime Minister Hwen Wu, with members of his cabinet, stood. Su-Mueng licked his lips nervously.

It had been his own idea: he would parade the cabinet of the Leisure Retort before his victorious soldiers. The venerable officials would lose face, would seem human and vulnerable. The workers would see for themselves the men who'd denied them their rights.

Hwen Wu, however, had been unexpectedly in favour of the confrontation. Indeed, he'd seemed not to understand Su-Mueng's intent, but had thanked him graciously for organising the proceeding. He should have been more forthright with Hwen Wu, Su-Mueng thought.

Because, in rolling, sonorous tones, the Prime Minister was praising the workers of the Production Retort for their timely intervention.

165

"Your sense of civil duty is gladdening to the heart," he said after a lengthy address, his aristocratic face impressively unreadable. "And now that the foreign barbarian has been driven out, we can all return to our allotted places and restore the perfect harmony of an ordered society."

He stepped back, folded his hands, smiled benignly upon Su-Mueng and upon the Production Retort managers who stood to one side, and retired to the rear of the balcony.

He's stolen the show, thought Sobrie. Poor Su-Mueng.

The managing director of the Production Retort came forward, inclined his head toward Hwen Wu, and then turned to speak a few polite words to the crowd, expressing his satisfaction at having served the city.

The workers gazed up at him with blank, curious faces. Everything was orderly and peaceful. With a shock Sobrie realised that they were going to return without argument to the Lower Retort, to their factories, their crude amusements.

The manager left the stage. Su-Mueng, Sobrie saw, was floundering. As a revolutionary, he was still a simpleton. He didn't have a clue as to how to effect social change: he thought it would happen of its own accord.

After hesitating, Su-Mueng took a step forward, but Sobrie overtook him and stepped into the centre of the crowd's attention.

What could he say that would begin the work of changing these people's minds? Of setting them on the course that would lead to equality between all men? Sobrie searched his mind, running through endless revolutionary texts, until he came to the most ancient evocation of all: one that was legendary, almost mythical, having been handed down since long before recorded history.

He raised his clenched fist. "Workers of the world, arise!" he began. "You have nothing to lose but your chains. . . ."

14.

Their footsteps echoed loudly in the big underground cavern. Planetary Leader Limnich, surrounded by aides and guards, was met just outside the door to the office complex by a tall, self-composed Colonel Brask.

"You got my message?" Limnich said after they'd saluted. "You understood its import?"

"I understood, Planetary Leader." Brask opened the door, inviting Limnich inside.

The Planetary Leader signalled his entourage to wait, then went in alone. Thankfully he settled himself in a deep leather armchair, as though exhausted. "You see why I had to contact you by code. Didn't want to trust vidphone transmissions with this . . . these days secrecy is becoming imperative. . . ."

He blinked, and then sniffed. He was feeling cold and shivery, but knew it was only his imagination, prompted by the knowledge that so many districts were down with the plague The virological laboratories were working desperately to combat the flood of new diseases that were appearing, almost certainly alien-caused, but as soon as one antibody was found another virus seemed to arise.

"Have you had time to confirm what you put in your message, Leader?" Brask asked him.

Limnich nodded. "It's true, all right. Whole regions have simply vanished off the map. Some new alien weapon, obviously, though the Mother knows what kind of device can annihilate people, buildings, and vegetation without leaving a trace. No radiation, nothing. Just bare soil."

"But it's mostly dev reservations that have vanished? Isn't that a little odd?"

Limnich shrugged. "Perhaps the aliens thought them convenient testing grounds. It isn't anything *we've* done, I can assure you of that. But you can see how serious the situation is. Is Measure C in hand?"

"Yes, Planetary Leader. The first wave will leave in a few minutes."

He switched on a large vidscreen. Limnich saw fine, upright men in time-combat suits, just marching away from their pre-flight ceremonies. He looked at them closely, admiring their courage, their dedication.

There was no time, now, to wait until the Legions of Kronos were up to the strength Limnich had wanted for the final assault. There was no time to build up the measures that would have given the warriors of time a fighting chance of personal survival. These were suicide crews, men who would battle through against all odds to drop their hydrogen bombs, scores of bombs to each ship. Something like his old feeling of reassurance came over Limnich as he looked on their stern resolve. Hours before, he knew, each man had donated sperm for freezing and storage, so that he'd be honoured with the knowledge that his seed would continue to contribute to the blood of the race.

"Excuse me, Planetary Leader, but in accordance with the protocol we've set up, I must ask to be allowed to leave you now."

Brask pressed a button. Another young officer came in – one more bright young man on which the Legions depended so much these days.

"Colonel Gole here will take over the project, as per your instructions, until the next wave is dispatched," Brask said.

Limnich gave a perfunctory nod, and Brask left with a final salute to them both.

The Planetary Leader continued to watch the screen as Brask took his place down below with his men. He watched the continuing ceremony as they boarded their time travellers, Brask taking the command ship.

"Eventually we'll find a way to bring them back alive," he said to Gole. "Until then, this is good enough."

"Yes, Planetary Leader."

The squadrons all vanished together with a sound like a thunderclap. They went humming fuzzily into the future, gladly bearing their cargoes of death, death, and more death.

Author's Note

The picture of time used as a background to this novel can be said to owe something to the discussions by J.W.Dunne, of *An Experiment With Time* fame, particularly from his book *The Serial Universe* where he sets forth the regression problem I describe in Chapter Nine.

The account of time I have chosen to derive from these arguments is, of course, a crude, fictionalised one, but it does manage to raise the question of whether the present moment is co-extensive throughout the universe, as Physicist Leard Ascar first believed, or whether it is a local process, as taught to him by the scientists of Retort City. I am inclined to imagine that the second version comes closer to the truth, though whether time is associated with biological systems, or with larger bodies such as galaxies, or with even larger structures such as, for instance, as much of the sidereal universe as would be observable from one point, is an open question.

B.J.B.